T   P

of

LIBERTY

Emergent Literatures

The
TRICKSTER
of
LIBERTY

TRIBAL HEIRS
to a
WILD BARONAGE

Gerald Vizenor (signature)

Gerald
VIZENOR

UNIVERSITY of MINNESOTA PRESS, Minneapolis

Published by the University of Minnesota Press
2037 University Avenue Southeast, Minneapolis MN 55414.
Published simultaneously in Canada
by Fitzhenry & Whiteside Limited, Markham.
Printed in the United States of America.

Original drawing (p. 6) by Karen Lohmann.

LIBRARY OF CONGRESS
Library of Congress Cataloging-in-Publication Data

Vizenor, Gerald Robert, 1934-
    The trickster of liberty : tribal heirs to a wild baronage /
Gerald Vizenor.
        p.   cm. — (Emergent literatures)
        ISBN 0-8166-1629-9 ISBN 0-8166-1630-2 (pbk.)
        I. Title. II. Series
    PS3572.I9T7 1988
    813'.54 — dc19   87-22167 CIP

In Memory of Joseph Vizenor

Contents

The Trickster, thus straddling oppositions, embodies two antithetical, nonrational experiences of man with the natural world, his society, and his own psyche: on the one hand, a force of treacherous disorder that outrages and disrupts, and on the other hand, an unanticipated, usually unintentional benevolence in which trickery is at the expense of inimical forces and for the benefit of mankind. . . . Myths are the agents of stability, fictions are the agents of change. Myths call for absolute, fictions for conditional assent.

Warwick Wadlington,
The Confidence Game in American Literature

Gerald VIZENOR

Prologue

TRICKSTERS and TRANSVALUATIONS

Sergeant Alex Hobraiser insisted that a white man posed as the naked brave on the Oregon Trail Memorial, a commemorative half dollar issued as a dubious tribute to those wild pioneers who crossed and then held tribal land; nonetheless, that contour could be an obverse trickster who won the last toss of the coin.

Alex leaned closer and pointed to the pectoral and deltoid muscles enhanced on the priapic warrior, a designer brave engraved in a cultural striptease. The sergeant spun the coin down a museum case and numismatic brawn overshadowed a covered wagon on the reverse side. Manifest destinies and sentimental histories were transvalued on a waver; the coin bounced, wobbled on the rim, and tricksters sallied in imagination. "There's a white hermaphrodite under that breechcloth," said the sergeant. "No one else would strip that way for fifty cents."

The Woodland trickster is a comic trope; a universal

language game. The trickster narrative arises in agonistic imagination; a wild venture in communal discourse, an uncertain humor that denies aestheticism, translation, and imposed representations. The most active readers become obverse tricksters, the waver of a coin in a tribal striptease.

The tribal trickster is a comic *holotrope*: the whole figuration; an unbroken interior landscape that beams various points of view in temporal reveries. The trickster is immortal; when the trickster emerges in imagination the author dies in a comic discourse. To imagine the tribal trickster is to relume human unities; colonial surveillance, monologues, and racial separations are overturned in discourse. "Imagination is not mere fancy," wrote George Lakoff in *Women, Fire, and Dangerous Things*, "for it is imagination, especially metaphor and metonymy, that transforms the general schemas defined by our animal experience into forms of reason. . . . "

The trickster is comic nature in a language game, not a real person or "being" in the ontological sense. Tribal tricksters are embodied in imagination and liberate the mind; an androgyny, she would repudiate translations and imposed representations, as he would bare the contradicitions of the striptease.

The trickster is lascivious, an erotic shimmer, a burn that sunders dioramas and terminal creeds; an enchanter, comic liberator, and word healer. The trickster mediates wild bodies and adamant minds; a chance in third person narratives to turn aside the cold litanies and catechistic monodramas over the measured roads to civilization. The implied author, narrators, the readers, listeners, and the characters, liven a comic and communal discourse.

Tribal tricksters arise in imagination, a comic discourse and language game. Narrative voices are corporeal in the oral tradition; on the other hand, translated trickster remain in printed words, summoned with passive news that holds gestures and wild names down to the number on the page. The translator imposes a worldview that sustains a monologue, a forfeiture of the language game.

The active reader implies the author, imagines narrative voices, inspires characters, and salutes tribal tricksters in a comic discourse; an erotic motion under the words absolves the separation between minds and bodies. The trickster is a "cosmic web" in imagination; we create our bodies with words, and there is a difference in each word. "Your body, the thing that seems most real to you, is doubtless the most phantasmatic," said Roland Barthes. "Perhaps it is even only phantasmatic. One needs an Other to liberate the body, but things become very difficult, and the result is all of philosophy, metaphysics, and psychoanalysis." The tribal trickster is another in the mind; our liberation in a comic discourse.

Jacques Lacan reasoned that what arises in language returns to language; words are ambiguous. "The word never has only one use," he said at a seminar. "Every word always has a beyond, sustains several meanings. Behind what discourse says, there is what it means . . . and behind what it wants to say there is another meaning, and this process will never be exhausted." Words, then, are metaphors and the trickster is a comic *holotrope*, an interior landscape "behind what discourse says." The trick, in seven words, is to *elude historicism, racial representations, and remain historical.* The author cedes the landscape to the reader and then dies, the narrators bear the schemes, bodies are wild, and the trickster liberates the mind in comic discourse.

Sergeant Alexina Hobraiser denies that she is a trickster, but she is, without a doubt, the best listener that ever lived on the reservation. "Trickster stories hit the mind, and our mind comes from animals not from our brain," she shouted. "So, when you listen to tricksters, listen with the mongrels."

Alex pushed the wheelchair closer to the low lancet windows. She lived with three mongrels in a library located behind the parish house and the old government school; a tribal concession to a woman warrior, a decorated and disabled veteran who told trickster stories.

"Mixedbloods are the best tricksters, the choice ticks on the tribal bloodline, like these mongrels on the porch," she said and laughed. White Lies and Chicken Lips snorted, pushed their wet noses hard on the screen door. Parastata, a cross between a black retriever and a basset hound, abandoned a birch tree and hobbled into the library on his short crooked forelegs; he smiled and mounted the anthropologist at the kitchen table. "Tricksters are wild children on the inside," she continued, "a red salute crossed with a white sparrow and a blue rose, one vast prairie that blooms on three hundred and thirteen words, exactly the number of panic holes a tribal trickster needs to be imagined in this wicked world."

"*Alexina*, why did you disown your given name?" asked the anthropologist. "Worried about being identified as a woman?" He smiled and opened his narrow hands over a notebook.

The sergeant turned to the window, pretended not to listen. "The trickster is never in a name, tribal tricksters are in our consciousness."

"You mean illusions," he countered.

"The sunrise is an illusion, the ocean is a trickster, and both are healers," said the sergeant. "Cesar Vallejo wrote that consciousness is that 'historical relationship between boat and water.' Our trickster is imagination, the humor between our minds and bodies, boats and water."

"Delusions and apologies," said the anthropologist as he gave the mongrels wide berth to the table. Parastata circled and mounted him from behind, crooked black forelegs around his knees.

Chicken Lips barked out the window at the crows over the parish house when the sergeant quoted N. Scott Momady, "We are what we imagine. Our very existence consists in our imagination of ourselves. . . . The greatest tragedy that can befall us is to go unimagined." The crows circled, landed on the parish road, and bounced in the dust.

"Momaday, of course, the most quoted and least read, but the question here is comic not tragic, and you cite elusive numbers, platitudes, and illusions to explain this tribal trickster," said the anthropologist. He moved around the table; a dialectic, he believed, was at hand. "What are some of these trickster words that heal like the sunrise?"

Alex was absolute and precise about the number of words, but she would never reveal tribal metaphors to an anthropologist with a research grant. "You're a paid word piler," she shouted and then turned in the wheelchair to tease the mongrels.

Eastman Shicer, cultural anthropologist and aerobics instructor, had recorded every sound she made last summer and then transcribed her words to discover what he believed was a "trickster code." The words she invented to distract the anthropologist became "primal signs" in his lexicon. He noted that "verbal nouns sustain her modern vision, unstable as that might seem as a sign; at the same time, we could hypothesize that the structure, mode, and the basic words in her stories are related more to her war experiences as a mixedblood than to a tribal oral tradition."

"Shicer, Shicer," the sergeant shouted from the seven windows of the library. "You listen too much with your ears, but listen, no one has a word hold on me, no one.

The trickster docks words not tails, crops manners not ears, because she's on the side of imagination and liberation, not termination, she's our last wild game, the toss of a coin in words, and you're nothing but a loss leader from the university."

Shicer was never at ease on the reservation; his academic tactics to harness the trickster in the best tribal narratives, and to discover the code of comic behavior, hindered imagination and disheartened casual conversations. The anthropologist would celebrate theories over imagination; in this sense, academic evidence was a euphemism for linguistic colonization of tribal memories and trickster narratives.

Paul Radin reviews the tribal trickster as the "presence of a figure" and as a "theme of themes" in various cultures. He declares that the trickster is a "creator and destroyer," and that he "knows neither good nor evil yet he is responsible for both. He possesses no values, moral or social, is at the mercy of his passions and appetites, yet through his actions all values come into being."

"The values, not the trickster, come into being," said the sergeant. "The trickster is a comic *holotrope* in a narrative, not a real person, but then neither are anthropologists." She pointed out that theories separated readers and tricksters, "cold separations from their visual memories."

Robert Pelton said that the trickster, ravenous and loutish, draws "order from ordure." He wrote that all "tricksters are foolers and fools, but their foolishness varies; sometimes it is destructive, sometimes creative, sometimes scatological, sometimes satiric, sometimes playful. In other words, the pattern itself is a shifting one, with now some, now others of the features presented."

Wendy Doniger O'Flaherty wrote that the trickster character represents a "coincidence of opposites far more general than androgyny. . . . The bitter humor with which he is depicted and the tragedy that follows upon his creative enterprises produce a sardonic vision of theological 'wholeness' and a satire on human sexual integration."

"Biological theories of sexuality, juridical conceptions of the individual, forms of administrative control in modern nations, led little by little to rejecting the idea of a mixture of the two sexes in a single body, and consequently to limiting the free choice of indeterminate individuals," wrote Michel Foucault in the introduction to *Herculine Barbin*. "Everybody was to have his or her primary, profound, determined and determining sexual identity; as for the elements of the other sex that might appear, they could only be accidental, superficial, or even quite simply illusory."

"Professor Carolyn Heilbrun," the sergeant continued, "wrote that the 'androgyny suggests a spirit of reconciliation between the sexes; it suggests, further, a full range of experience open to individuals who may, as women, be aggressive, as men, tender; it suggests a spectrum upon which human beings choose their places without regard to propriety or custom.' The trickster arises in imagination and integrates sexual distinctions in narratives."

Shicer cleared his throat and asked Alexina, "Have you, by chance, ever read Richard Wilhelm's brilliant lectures on the *Book of Changes*?" White Lies moaned and pushed her wet nose into his crotch.

"Yes, by chance," she responded.

"Excellent," he said and crossed his legs. "Wilhelm points out that 'the presence of opposites is necessary for experience to take place. There must be contrast between subject and object, for otherwise consciousness, or the knowledge of things, is altogether impossible' and that, it must be said, is true when we examine the tricksters."

"Opposites are never the opposite," the sergeant shouted. "Why must you turn the trickster into an anthropological cat's cradle?"

"Absolutely," said the anthropologist. "Wilhelm said that the opposites are not enduring, but they 'should be seen as changing states, which can pass from one into another.' He also wrote that 'opposites provoke one another, and for this very reason they can be made to harmonize.' You see then that one way to understand the trickster is to discover his opposites." The black mongrel mounted the anthropologist once more. Parastata, ravished with priapism, mounts and humps whatever is upright and pretentious. Shicer would have been much more embarrassed in the academic world where an erection is ruined with no humor.

"*Her* opposition," the sergeant demanded.

"Of course, *her* opposites."

"She opposes anthropologists, she said, "because you are a method, and your methods are the death of imagination and the end of the trickster. The trickster is a communal voice in a comic worldview, not a tragic method in the social sciences, and the trickster needs ten times more lust to overcome your inhibitions to even imagine the world. Chicken Lips barked and White Lies howled at the anthropologist.

"Who would you be without an anthropologist?

"You and your tragic theories, the sergeant continued, "separate life from death and love from hate, because you're an academic monologue, an autistic recitation with the delusions that the world is structured in your heroic and isolated brain.

"That's brilliant, said the anthropologist as he reached for his tape recorder. Chicken Lips licked his hands and the dark hair on his arms. Parastata mounted White Lies under the table.

"Have you, by chance, ever read *And Our Faces,*

My Heart Brief as Photos by John Berger?" asked the sergeant. She pushed her wheelchair to the bookcase. White Lies barked and bounced in a circle.

"You imagined that title?"

"Berger wrote that the 'opposite of to love is not to hate but to separate. If love and hate have something in common it is because, in both cases, their energy is that of bringing and holding together—the lover with the loved, the one who hates with the hated. Both passions are tested by separation.' "

Carl Gustav Jung said the trickster was a "collective shadow figure, an epitome of all the inferior traits of character in individuals. And since the individual shadow is never absent as a component of personality, the collective figure can construct itself out of it continually. . . . He is both subhuman and superhuman, a bestial and divine being, whose chief and most alarming characteristic is his unconsciousness. . . . In the history of the collective as in the history of the individual, everything depends on the development of consciousness. This gradually brings liberation from imprisonment. . . . "

"Shadows, consciousness, and liberation," the sergeant said to the mongrels, "there you have our tribal trickster and the best tickets to the language games."

"Three more words?" asked Shicer.

"In literature or in ecology, comedy enlightens and enriches human experience without trying to transform either mankind or the world," wrote Joseph Meeker in *The Comedy of Survival.* "The comic mode of human behavior represented in literature is the closest art has come to describing man as an adaptive animal."

Beat moved her wheelchair to the south windows where the traceries bound the light in primal bows. "The trickster is embodied in imagination, we see rainbows at certain angles to the sun and earth, but we are never seen in the places we see, or what we see is never what we choose to see, and the trickster is a lure beyond our gaze."

"Anamorphosis," said the anthropologist.

"*Jouissance*," she responded.

"Shit, and clever delights," he retorted.

"Shicer, you're a sign consumer, but you got the first word on my list," said the sergeant as she wheeled to the shadows in the corner of the room. White Lies sneezed twice at Parastata.

"Shit, or the sign?"

"One down, three hundred and twelve more panic holes to go, but you're talking in the wrong places." Chicken Lips circled the wheelchair and snapped at black flies.

"Generally speaking," said Jacques Lacan, "the relation between the gaze and what one wishes to see involves a lure. The subject is presented as other than he is, and what one shows him is not what he wishes to see. . . . In any picture, it is precisely in seeking the gaze in each of its points that you will see it disappear."

The tribal trickster eludes our common gaze, a lure in a comic *holotrope*; she is neither blessed nor evil, neither real nor a transformation, but in wild traceries he wavers on the rim, a warrior on a coin that never lands twice on the same side. "This is the way the world begins, this is the way the world begins," the sergeant chanted, "this is the way the world begins, not with an anthropologist but with mongrels and tricksters in a language game."

The
TRICKSTER
of
LIBERTY

The BARON
of PATRONIA

Luster Browne shouted at the birch behind the parish house; he revered the bright woods, but not so white, and not so close to the missionaries. He bashed the weeds and threw his words at the white posse on the back porch of the mission.

Luster was there at dawn, a mixedblood at the scratch line, to disrupt the land allotment measures on the White Earth Reservation in northern Minnesota. He prowled behind the birch and sneered at the federal agents on the porch; later, tired and lonesome, he abided the distance with the mongrels and became a nobleman.

That comic moment reared a compassionate tribal trickster, nurtured his wild children and nine grandchildren, and overturned an instance in racial hocus-pocus on that woodland reservation, which was invented in eighteen sixty-eight by withered white men in cutaway coats.

Luster renounced the strict summons to mature in a base and possessive civilization, and he would never wait on a mission porch to have his mind mended by the government, even when his mind needed mending. The trickster seceded at dawn behind the bridal wreath; he pissed on the birch with the mongrels and countered the breach in communal tribal land. In response, he was handed a land patent that banished him to the wild outback on the reservation.

"Luster Browne, also known as Lusterbow, his callow moniker, son of a pagan mother and a mixed father, a common factor in the fur trade, comes hitherward for his allotment, the last holdover on this reservation roll," the government clerk announced in a taut monotone. "Howbeit, the halfbreed has lost favor with the mission and our agents."

The assistant secretary, braced high in a chair behind a bench overspread with a martial blanket, scorned the recalcitrant mixedblood when he issued a certificate in his name. The untamed land between the metes and bounds ascribed, the secretary believed, was impenetrable muskeg, as worthless as the peerage he pronounced that humid afternoon in the name of the president.

"Whereas, there has been deposited in the General Land Office of the United States an Order of the Secretary of the Interior directing that a fee simple patent issue to Luster Browne, a White Earth Mississippi Chippewa Indian, for a quarter west of the Fifth Principal Meridian containing one-hundred sixty acres in a Township named Patronia:

"Now know ye, that the United States of America, in consideration of the promises, has given and granted, and by these presents does give and grant, unto the said Luster Browne, and to his heirs, the lands above described, and the title, Baron of Patronia; to have and to hold the same, together with all the rights, privileges, immunities, and appurtenances, of whatsoever nature thereunto belonging, unto the said Baron Luster Browne, and to his heirs and assigns forever.

"In testimony whereof, I, Theodore Roosevelt, President of the United States of America, have caused these letters to be made Patent, and the seal of the General Land Office to be hereunto affixed."

The malevolent assistant secretary, however, was mistaken about the worth of the land he had allotted to the mixedblood trickster; the baronage, intended to be a colonial hoax, became a virtue in one generation, and the heritable tribal noblesse has prevailed in various ancestral comedies, here and there, and on the reservation.

Patronia is a wild crescent on the White Earth Reservation northeast of Bad Medicine Lake. The shallow creek at the treeline carries the last rumors of glacial rivers that once tumbled the huge granite boulders down the hollows; there, the greens are tender in the spring.

A weathered hutment bears down behind the cedar on the west bank of the creek; white pine and a rush of paper birch hold between the boulders on the slow rise of the crescent. Thousands of moccasin orchids bloom in the moist summer shadows.

The sunrise widens on the other side of the creek, over emerald waves, blood hues, and wild blues, on a natural meadow; insects swarm in humid columns, and at night, fireflies leave their traceries in the moist weeds.

In a warm pond, on the northern brow of the wild crescent, mallards remain in winter; their green heads and brown bodies cross in the mist between the reeds, between the children on the luscious shore.

The Baron of Patronia camped behind the cedars that first summer and built a small cabin near the pond. When the rime turned the leaves and the blues withered on the meadow, he cut whitewood for the winter; later, when

6   Gerald VIZENOR

the mallards waited on the warm water, he married an orphan who lived in a wigwam over the meadow at Long Lost Lake.

Novena Mae Ironmoccasin was born premature in a wild snow storm on Advent Sunday. The unmarried mother died from exposure behind the mission. The Benedictine sisters at the White Earth boarding school cared for the child; when she recovered and opened her eyes for the first time on the ninth day of their prayers in eighteen ninety-two, the nuns named her for the novena. She was a dark and silent child, a serious student, and devoted to the sisters at the mission, but she turned down a summons to become a nun. Instead, when she was fifteen, she created a wild Stations of the Cross on fourteen wounded trees behind the mission, and then she retreated to the hardwoods.

She was sixteen when the second winter loomed on the mound and a lone trickster wandered close to her wigwam. Crows roused the red pine, wind rushed the cattails, beaver cracked the thin ice on the riverside; these motions she understood. But over these natural sounds that late autumn she heard several splendid wild human shouts.

The Baron of Patronia came over the meadow and buried his lonesome voice in seven panic holes; there, he believed, the overturned earth would nurture wild flowers with his words, in his noble name. He planted his voice, in this manner, with the seasons: in summer with the moccasin orchids, his solace bloom; on the meadow in spring and autumn; under the cedar in winter.

Novena Mae watched him move between shadows; she was hushed and courteous at the treeline. He was sudden; his breath was wild, blanched, blued on the tender rise. The mongrels raised their wet noses on the wind, sensed her presence, but the trickster was not aware that she had tracked him more than a mile back across the meadow to his baronage, down to his cedar cabin on the pond.

Lusterbow shouted and circled the pond, but she remained silent and held her distance. The mallards browsed on the warm water between them. He recited poesies on the weather, ducks in winter, rimes on the wild wind over warm water, and the moss down the crescent to the pond, and then he told trickster stories about hibernal bears and the colossus icewoman who consumed lonesome men in winter.

"Woman, come over here," he shouted and danced on the shore. The mongrels bounced in the weeds, searched in wild circles for new panic holes, and then barked at the baron. "The Baron of Patronia, he is me, and he welcomes you to live on his land, as long as the grass grows, the river flows." He laughed, waved his hands, and then silence. "Would you be the icewoman?"

Novena Mae remained silent; she smiled and rolled a shoulder when the crows and whiskey jacks responded to his loud voice. He shouted several more humorous invitations; the bewildered mongrels barked at his shadow, made their own panic holes, and then moved to the other side of the pond.

Later, when it was dark, he built a fire on the shore and announced that he would wait there for her response. When he leaned back, a solemn shadow in the weeds, she teased the mongrels and returned to her wigwam on the mound. There she touched a blue stone bear that her mother wore when she died in the storm; she listened and remembered the nuns at the mission, the wounded trees, and counted the months that she had been alone. She remembered each month in scent and sound: the harsh cracks on the lake ice, mice in the dried oak leaves, blue mire overturned in winter, black bears on the river boulders, water striders in a warm rain, lightning in the white pine, and her heart beat under moss, in cold river water. She would never be ruined with these memories; she would be mocked but never ruined by a tribal trickster.

Novena Mae untied the birchbark wigwam, packed several bundles on a small travois, and towed her possessions back across the meadow and down to the warm pond. Lusterbow snored low in the weeds; the cedar embers hissed, snapped, and danced over his head.

The mongrels were the overseers that night when she tied the larch poles and re-covered her wigwam with bark. She spread woven rushes and cedar boughs inside. The entrance opened on the creek and the best sunrise. She listened to the water resound over the stones and then made a small fire in the center of the wigwam.

The Baron of Patronia awakened with a shiver and stirred the cedar embers. Overhead, mythic hunters spread their scarlet pennons on the dawn; the autumn meadow shimmered and the paper birch on the crescent were rose-hued. He moved closer, mongrels in the lead, to the wigwam. When he peered inside, his shadow covered her head and chest. She was curled near the fire; thin, even smaller than he had imagined from the other side of the pond. She wore a leather blouse, laced under the sleeves and buttoned down the sides, wide cotton trousers, and leather leggings. He moved back to watch the dawn reach over her neck and cheeks; when her nose hitched, he retreated to his cabin.

Lusterbow leaned on the window sash and brooded over his isolation; then he marched down to the warm pond to bathe and wash his pungent clothes.

Chicken Lips, the most curious of the two mongrels, hopped around inside the wigwam; he sniffed her hair, her feet, and then pushed his wet nose into her crotch. When she awakened he sneezed and lost his balance, rolled over on the cedar boughs. Chicken Lips was mottled brown with three wide white paws; the right front paw had been severed in a beaver trap.

White Lies was seated at the entrance. She was white with brown blotches and with narrow bands on her stout tail; brown wisps shrouded her rear. She moaned, licked her sides, and snapped at a slow insect. The mongrels were more at home in the wigwam than on the rough boards in the cabin.

Novena Mae and Lusterbow never lived in the same house; he remained in the cedar cabin he had built near the pond, and she lived in the wigwam where she delivered ten children in twelve years. She was wild, generous, hushed; he was wild, bounteous, hoarse. He screamed the names of his children over panic holes on the meadow; she marked the birth of her children on the hardwoods and taught them to read from leaves. She wrote words and names on leaves and scattered them on the hard snow; the children collected the leaves and told stories with random words, their words, their voices on the rise.

Lusterbow told wild stories, trickster and creation stories, and coached his children to scream into panic holes when the spirit moved them. The meadow was covered with wild blooms, nurtured with screams; even the mongrels barked into holes and covered their sound with the earth. He was in motion when he told stories, never at rest; he worked with cedar, or he walked and talked, and waved his beaver stick between phrases.

Lusterbow built small cedar cabins for each of his children, an enormous barn near the pond, and several other buildings for sheep, mongrels, and dead machines issued by the government; when he worked he told stories about tribal tricksters who lived in compasses, clocks, watches, and church organs, where the best of them recast tunes, overturned time, and reversed magnetic directions in the manifest white world. The children learned apace to listen and then to imagine their connections to the earth; each child earned a characteristic nickname and a comic temper to endure the ruthless brokers of a tragic civilization.

The children learned that the old tribal tricksters turned "rose window malevolence" into comic beams and enlightened those who had lost their shadows on the concrete.

Shadow Box Browne, the eldest son, and his two unmarried sisters remained with their parents, Luster and Novena Mae, at Patronia. The other seven children moved to small communities on the reservation; two were reconciled in cities. Rain Browne and her brother Bones studied art and distinguished themselves as painters: he was a romantic and a tribal naturalist, she was a hard expressionist. Swarm, the eldest daughter, had vanished in a thunder storm when she was twelve; two sons, the smallest and the most intrepid of the children, had died in a cloud of mustard gas over a narrow trench in the Great War.

Shadow Box married Wink Martin, his cousin, who lived with her brother, Mouse Proof, at Bad Medicine Lake. Wink was silent but never solemn. She was stout and her breath was bad; she covered her mouth with one hand to hide her rotten teeth. She winked when she listened, and double winked when she smiled. Wink counted and measured words with winks; she even winked to count her children, the cabins, the mongrels, the mallards on the pond, and the crows on the blue meadow. She winked over the panic holes but never learned to scream.

Lusterbow built a cedar cabin for each grandchild, two more for Mouse Proof Martin, who would not leave his sister, and one cabin for Griever de Hocus, the avian trickster from Bad Medicine Lake. When his children and grandchildren were grown and the cabins weathered in silence,

Lusterbow invited street tricksters, those with docked visions, mixedbloods from the cities, to live at Patronia. Three remained, learned his stories, and built their own cabins; the other mixedbloods screamed once into a panic hole and then braced their boredom at the Last Lecture, the nearest tavern, where they subscribed to new names and renewed indentities.

Mouse Proof Martin moved with his sister and established a new museum in the two cabins that the Baron of Patronia had built for him near the pond. Mouse Proof earned his nickname at a federal boarding school, where, on his hands and knees, he learned to read and write under an organ console. He waited, with one slack ear, at the narrow feet of his teacher when she played the organ in the classroom. There, on the bellows pedals, the two words of his nickname were pressed in metal. Mouse Proof turned under the organ and looked up her dress, into her dark crotch, as she perched on the stool. Then, with one finger, he traced the deep letters in the two words on the base of the pedals. He carved these words on his battered wooden desk, he wounded trees with his written name, and he painted his name on the new water tower.

Mouse Proof secured his name on the reservation, but he was better known as the trickster who collected lost and autographed shoes. His wild obsession with shoes started at the feet of his teacher; the smell of white flesh and polished leather. Later, when he found lost shoes at the roadside, he would remember his teacher, the scent of her crotch and shoes, and the unusual origin of his name. He owned thousands of lost shoes, each one catalogued, covered with a sock, and stored in his cabin archives. Once each season he scheduled tours to various institutions and museums with a selection of his rare shoe collection.

Mouse Proof and his wild shoe stories were popular on college campuses; he animated the lonesome shoes, moved them in uncommon pairs, uncovered their character and precise wear, and imagined in stories what happened to the shoes that never got away, the shoes that were never lost. The children adored his stories about lost and lonesome shoes.

Griever de Hocus roamed with Mouse Proof Martin and told stories about meditation and broken wheels to college audiences. Griever was born without a name, the child of a caravan called the Universal Hocus Crown. His mother told him that she met his father at three places on the reservation. Once in the birch behind the parish house, twice on the old government road, and three times in the ice barn near the lake; and then, "the caravan and your father, gone in less than a week." She never even learned his real name, never understood his peculiar language, but she remembers his tongue, his music, and she whistles his wild tunes at night; most of all, she remembers what he said about "griever time."

"Griever time meditation," he told her in the dark, "cures common colds, headaches, heartaches, tired feet, and humdrum blood." The caravan sold plastic icons with grievous poses, miniature grails, veronicas, and instruction manuals entitled How To Be Sad And Downcast And Still Live In Better Health Than People Who Pretend To Be So Happy. She owes her old age to "griever time meditation" three nights a week. Griever owes his name and humor to her compulsive lamentations, but not much more. Mouse Proof and Griever de Hocus met under the organ console and were close friends at boarding school.

Wink Browne covered her mouth with both hands, counted nine children, her husband, brother, and stopped on eleven winks. "No more," she whispered, "no more bad breath," and she uncovered an enormous cast of ceramic teeth. Mormons provided the teeth, an inducement to their religion. Wink smiled at the missionaries twice a week for three months, an estimate of the value, and then she returned to the old mission and the mean deacon with the winy breath; instead of winking she clicked her teeth. Wink was so pleased with her smile that she traveled with her brother, Mouse Proof, and his shoe collection to several museum shows.

Shadow Box counted cabins and names marked on the trees near the pond. China, he shouted, his first born daughter; Tune, his eldest son; Tulip, the detective; Garlic, the farmer; Ginseng, the root rustler; Eternal Flame, once a nun; Father Mother, once a priest; Mime, who imitated her mother; and Slyboots, the avian dreamer and microlight radical.

China was born when the clover and rue anemone were in bloom on the meadow. Shadow Box roared with the scarlet hunters that morning; the mongrels circled the cabin and barked at their loose shadows. Lusterbow shouted in a panic hole to celebrate the birth of his first grandchild.

Chicken Lips waited at the bedside and whined over the child. He mocked her babble, and then he licked her little pink feet. He pushed his smooth tongue between her moist toes; the more she moved her toes, the more he licked.

White Lies and Chicken Lips, namesake mongrels, inherited their names; seven mongrels barked into panic holes on the meadow, withered, and died, but their names were resurrected in each generation. Patronia children remember the same mongrel names in their tribal stories.

China Browne teased Chicken Lips when she was

older; she would spread her toes to catch his smooth tongue. Later she pretended that her feet were bound, golden lotuses under blue bandannas, and the mongrels were her eunuchs. Lusterbow claimed that he heard the echo of her name when he shouted into a panic hole, down to the other side of the earth, to the other world.

China studied literature, the first child from the baronage to graduate from college, and she traveled around the world as a magazine writer. Chicken Lips came to mind whenever she was lonesome or insecure; she would remember the reservation and that warm mongrel tongue between her toes. Now, once or twice a week, she draws silk ribbons between her toes; an unusual meditation, and the certain origin of her nickname.

Tune Browne, the eldest grandchild on the baronage, bears a nickname that was once used in a phrase: Tune In, Tune Out, Tune Up, Call the Tune, and A Different Tune. He is remembered on the reservation as the trickster with the most unusual tunes. Tune wore an enormous tricorne when he told stories; he said he once lived in a museum with Ishi, the last survivor of the Yahi tribe. Tune established the New School of Socioacupuncture at the University of California at Berkeley.

Tulip Browne reveals no secrets and bears no reservation nostomania. She is a trickster, a private detective, and she is obsessed with wind, with natural power; the moon, mountains, bears, crows, but not men, seldom men. Two new windmills whir on the crescent over the pond, and when she constructed them the baronage was powered into the modern world. Now the ocean wind whirs on miniature windmills in her condominium. Tulip, the name she uses as a detective, is shortened from Tulipwood, a nickname that described the colors of her skin when she was a child. Her cheeks were translucent at birth, rose-hued like the birch at dawn, and her hands held wild natural colors. She earned her nickname from the streaks of color in the light wood of the tulip tree.

Garlic Browne was born with a passion to eat garlic; as a child he hunted the wild bulbous lilies, washed the cloves in the warm pond, and then chewed them raw. White Lies, the mongrel with broken canines, was the second best garlic eater on the reservation; he even retrieved cloves thrown in the pond. Garlic studied agricultural sciences, and with government loans he developed the mammoth Patronia Garlic and became the most prosperous garlic grower in the state; sovereign garlic on the baronage. Then, late one summer, in the prime of his garlic career, he was struck by lightning on the meadow; he was buried where he died, in his own panic hole.

Ginseng Browne was born with an instinct to unearth wild ginseng in the hardwoods. His trade agreements with the People's Republic of China wavered when he was indicted on a federal warrant; the trickster was accused of stealing mature ginseng seeds from a commercial grower with the intent to violate the Convention of International Trade in Endangered Species of Fauna and Flora, a treaty ratified to protect plant and animal species. The China National Medicines and Health Products Import and Export Corporation established a mission on the baronage and promised to erect the Trickster of Liberty, an enormous statue on the meadow, in return for an exclusive contract to buy wild amber ginseng.

Eternal Flame Browne renounced the convent and established a scapehouse on the baronage. Sister Flame, the most sensitive nun in the order, earned her name at the cloister; the abbess noticed her natural blush and read the wild passion in her letters. The Patronia Scapehouse is a haven to wounded women; near the entrance there are four booths where the scapehouse women listen to the confessions of reservation men.

Father Mother Browne renounced the priesthood and ordained the Last Lecture, a tavern and sermon center, at a watershed to the south of the baronage. The Edge of the Earth, a low stone precipice, stands behind the Last Lecture; on the edge there are seven public telephone booths. Those who subscribed to go over the edge were allowed one free call before they dropped into their new names and identities. Father Mother, a name he earned as a child because he could never decide if he wanted to become a mother or a father, heard confessions at the Last Lecture; he invited urban mixedbloods, and those who were lost and lonesome, to choose new names and drop over the edge into a new world.

Mime Browne was born with no palate; the sounds she uttered were never understood, so she learned to mouth silent words and to imitate hand and facial gestures. The gestures of her brothers and sisters changed when they learned to imitate the people they wanted to become. Mime tried her grandfather and then decided to become her mother; her imitation was so adroit that her mother was embarrassed. Mime continued to wink when her mother turned to the click of her new teeth. The night after her brother died in a lightning storm on the meadow, she was raped and murdered behind the mission.

Slyboots Browne, the most devious, clever, and artful of the tricksters at the baronage, is a wild avian dreamer who assumes, surmises, and imagines a world with no halters. Slyboots attended private schools and graduated from Dartmouth College where he learned how to write proposals and fly a biplane. When he returned to the reservation, he proposed to build microlight airplanes with an economic development grant, but federal agents ruled that aviation was a "frivolous" tribal enterprise and the plan was denied. Slyboots rallied with a down-to-earth proposal to manufacture the Microlight Muskeg Rover, a universal terrain vehicle that would crawl through the snow and muck on remote reservations. The federal agents were impressed with his practical invention. When no one bought the land vehicles and the scheme died, Slyboots salvaged the equipment, converted the engines, and built his own airplane, the Patronia Microlight. Later, in the barn near the pond, he turned out two microlights each week and trained tribal pilots for an airborne revolution.

The Baron of Patronia died over a panic hole in the mocassin orchids and was buried high on the meadow with two mongrels. His voice is heard on cold winter nights. Novena Mae lived to be more than a hundred and died in a dream at a riverside in autumn. She was buried on the mound near her original wigwam at Long Lost Lake.

Shadow Box and Wink remained at the baronage; he became the maintenance man at the Patronia Scapehouse, and she waited on tables at the Last Lecture. Their children, the mixedblood heirs to a wild tribal baronage, convene in stories; the narratives show their compassion and imaginative transactions as tricksters.

Griever de Hocus, an adopted heir to the baronage, said that woodland tricksters were "heart gossipers" with no more to win or lose than a blush. "We are more than a curious medicine bundle on a museum rack," he told a college audience when he was on a lonesome shoe tour with Mouse Proof Martin. "We are tricksters in the blood, natural mixedblood tricksters, word warriors in that silence between bodies, and we bear our best medicine on our voices, in our stories.

"Watch me now," he said and smiled. The trickster

moved backward, an avian pass on the polished rostrum. "The trickster heals with humor and wonder, we wear the agonistic moment, not the burdens of the past, but beware," he said and frowned, "in our second stories we turn the mood, liberate chickens, autistic colonists, and overthrow the world that you remember, and learn to count on the clock."

CHINA BROWNE

RED STARS
and BOUND LILIES

China Browne waited with the privileged cadre in the new railroad station lounge. She trimmed her nails and looked over pictures in a news magazine; she would not touch her bare arms or neck to the couch because the leather was stained and smelled of garlic sweat.

Two men in uniform smoked and whispered at the counter near the entrance to the lounge; a man in a thin white shirt wheezed in a corner chair, his stout arms surrounded a plastic briefcase with a broken zipper. Enormous fans whirred near the door to the latrine and circulated the noisome stench of urine.

China smiled as she read the faded broadsides on the wall over the counter, travel legends overrun with advertisements and cautions: China, A Treasure In The Heart; See Tibet With Two Big Eyes; Make Wind On A Phoenix Bicycle; Chemicals Not To Travel The Trains; No Spit The Floor; Monkey King Opera; No Spit The Street.

Outside, in the main section of the train station, tired women hunkered over their children and cloth bundles; the men smoked and watched foreigners. Some families, in spite of the heat, cooked on charcoal braziers; elders heated water for tea. The pollution beclouded the patriotic portraits high on the walls in the station.

An American couple, a mock blonde and her bearded husband, rushed into the lounge and collapsed, breathless, on the leather couch. She counted their parcels and suitcases, retied a carton wrapped with newspaper, and then she fanned her neck and measured the other people in the lounge. The two men in uniform moved closer to read the headlines on her carton, the folded pictures of four men convicted of rape and sentenced to death.

"Angel and me are teachers here, this is our second year," said the bearded man in a loud voice, "we thought it might be easier the second time around with some experience, but maybe not, who are you?"

"China Browne."

"Angel, this is China Browne," he said and dried his beard with a hand towel. "Well then, you must be part Chinese."

"Native American," she said with a smile and waited for the characteristic responses, the racial catechism, questions about reservations, religion, language, and tribal radicals in prison.

"Aren't we all?"

"Native American Indian."

"Like I said, aren't we all," said Angel.

"Make up your mind," he said.

"China like in China?" asked Angel. When she leaned forward her white thighs squeaked on the dark leather. "Where did you ever get a name like that?"

"From my father," whispered China.

"Cinch is my nickname," he announced.

"China is mine."

"My father said making me was a cinch, the easiest thing he ever did that ended up paid to travel and talk in a classroom," boasted Cinch.

"China comes to China," mused Angel. "Where are you going in this awful, awful heat?" She mopped her short hair and withered neck with a towel; rouge and other cosmetic hues were smeared on her cheeks.

China was prepared to respond when a woman in a blue uniform propped open the double doors and announced the departure of the train to Tianjin. China nodded to Angel and then shouldered her overnight pack.

Children churred in the wide corridor of the station; women washed their babies on the aisle, and toddlers pissed on the terrazzo. Cinch and Angel plodded through the crowd with their parcels.

"China, you're my kind of woman."

"How is that?"

"You travel light." Cinch carried three suitcases and a backpack. "There are no porters here, not since the revolution, you can be sure."

"Liberation here, burden there," mocked China.

"Where is your luggage?" asked Angel.

"Beijing Hotel."

"So, you've been here how long?"

"Three days, long enough to catch my breath."

"Here, carry this then, you need something in your hands to be with us." Angel handed her the carton wrapped with newspaper which was much heavier than the suitcases; the coarse rope cut into her fingers.

China pressed through the narrow turnstile behind an old woman with bound feet. The woman was dressed in loose blue trousers, a black blouse, and a brown shroud on her shoulders; she wore a visor cap with a red ceramic star on the front cocked back on her head like a soldier.

China was pushed down the stairs, butted with baskets and hard bundles. She slowed the press from behind so the old woman could hobble at her own speed down to the platform; there, when the woman stopped near the tracks in a patch of light and held a rail ticket close to one eye, China moved closer to her side, turned, and smiled. The woman covered the ticket with both hands, as if her destination were a state secret, and stared at the nose on the foreigner; then the old peasant woman lowered her head in silence.

China bowed, bundled her hands between her breasts and spoke in Chinese: "China Browne is my name," she said in measured tones. "I am an American."

The old woman wobbled to the side on her golden lilies and dropped her cloth bundle. China reached down to retrieve the bundle, but the old woman shivered, waved her arms, and dropped her ticket; she moved over the ragged cloth, raised her head, and shouted, "Yang gui zi, yang gui zi," which means, "foreign devil."

China moved back when a crowd gathered around her on the platform. The woman shouted that the foreign devil had spied on her, tried to read her ticket and steal her clothes. The men smoked and watched the scene in silence; the women in the crowd repeated in whispers what the old woman had shouted.

"China, never mind, Mao's still on her mind," said Cinch. "There's nothing you can do or say, best to count your change and move on with the other foreign devils."

"Love that star on her hat," said China. She brushed her hair back, smiled, and pretended not to be troubled by the occurrence.

"We've been here a year and we still don't under-

24   Gerald VIZENOR

stand," said Angel, "so don't get your hopes up in three days. Best to ignore the old people unless they seek you out, nothing comes of trying to help people here, they won't even help each other."

"Estranged, and with no porters," muttered China.

"Right, that's the ticket," said Cinch. He moved their suitcases to cover a particular crack on the platform; there, he explained, "is where the soft seat coach will stop, right on the crack, right on time."

The old woman hobbled down the platform to a place she knew the "hard seat" coach would stop; crowded, unreserved, right on the mark. She waited with her head raised, her mouth puckered.

China would overturn mistrust and suspicion on the baronage, back on the reservation, with tribal trickeries; however, she was a foreign devil cornered in a hard-core diorama with no natural cues to the humor in the nation. Men stared at her breasts, that was not new, and the children watched her shoes; the women whispered about the prominence of her nose and the criminals pictured on the carton that she carried. The locomotive thundered into the station and steam smothered the curious crowd on the platform.

Cinch sat on the aisle, sipped green tea, and commented on each crossroad, hamlet, lime mine, and new advertisement on the sides of buildings between Beijing and Tianjin. When the train arrived, he was on the platform in seconds; he maneuvered through the crowded station and onto the main street. Angel ran close behind and complained the whole distance.

China, meanwhile, waited in the station to see the old peasant woman once more; she hobbled alongside a couple with an automatic washer in an enormous carton tied to a bicycle. The old woman waited at the curb outside the station for a few minutes; she raised her head several times and then hobbled across the wide street, oblivious to the trucks and buses. She paused on the other side, raised her head, and turned down to the river. The bank was stepped with rough concrete. Children swam into the black water from the last tier; women spread their washed clothes on the concrete.

The old woman inched down the bank, side to side on her narrow bound feet. The tiers were crowded with people; hundreds were at the waterline to cool their bodies on the breeze over the river.

China leaned back on a tier high above the water and watched the children, the old woman, and the boats loaded with bales. She remembered the baronage, the cedar, and her grandmother, who lived in a wigwam near the river; the old woman invited the mongrels to lick her toes when she was a child. China whispered her name there on the stepped bank, "Novena, Novena Mae," and the names of the mongrels, "Chicken Lips," and "White Lies." She imagined that Chicken Lips pressed his wet nose on her toes, turned his tongue between her toes. China removed her shoes, spread her toes on the rough concrete, and prepared to meditate; however, when she drew the blue bandanna from her shoulder pack, the old woman stumbled over a seam on the last tier and bounced into the water. The woman was desperate, she held her arms and shoulders above water, but she was weak, her hands trembled on the concrete.

China was thirteen tiers above the river; she waited for someone to help the old woman. There were people near her, but no one seemed to notice. Her bound lotus feet bobbed in the dark water, stunted creatures from the imperial past.

China shouted and waved with her shoes to those below; when no one responded, she bounded down the tiers. She eased the old woman back from the water and rested her head on the shoulder pack. The woman shivered on the concrete; she moved to hide her feet, and her cloth bundle, under the shroud. The two women watched each other in silence; one smiled and then the other.

China raised the wet shroud and spread it on the concrete tiers to dry. She unbound the old woman, loosened the swathes, uncovered her feet. China opened the tender wizened toes like secrets and cleaned the pinched ocherous nails; the lotus toes were more erotic than she had imagined, more beauteous than the pictures of bound feet she treasured as a child. She dried the turned toes with her blue bandanna, the same cloth she drew between her own toes in meditation.

The cicadas roared in the broad leaves, and boat whistles sounded on the river; diesel engines bellowed over the bridge in the distance. China drowsed and children dabbled in the water on the tier below her head. She dreamed that her grandfather floated past on a boat and told stories about the mixedblood trickster who lived in a town clock. The trickster read the minds of those who looked to the tower for their time, and he set the hands back to calm their nerves. Lusterbow said that when the trickster moved the hands on the tower clock, the time in the whole town moved back; this, he mused, was the pleasure of a compassionate tribal trickster.

China awakened when the boat passed and the stories ended. The old woman had bound her toes and waited with her cloth bundle at her side. China shouldered her pack and the two women climbed the tiers together. China narrated the rise with the origin of her name and the baronage on the reservation. The old woman did not respond, she was out of breath and did not seem to hear the stories.

China ushered the woman to a wooden bench that overlooked the river. There, beneath a tree, she shouted into a panic hole and the old woman understood; she smiled, nodded, and bowed, and then she clapped her withered hands. China shouted a second time into the seared earth.

"Yang gui zi," she whispered, and then laughed louder than she had shouted earlier on the platform. The old woman leaned over and presented a small herb box and her cloth cap to the foreign devil on the bench beside her; she polished the red star, bowed twice more, and hobbled down the road. China watched the old woman cross the bridge; she vanished in the crowd.

Cinch was irritated that the time in his measured world had been disturbed by China. He marched to the back of the bench and shouted in her ear: "Where have you been? We've been looking all over the place for you, now we're late." She was taken unawares and twitched with his voice; when she turned he circled the bench. He pulled his beard as he marched, then he stopped and waited for her response.

"Two o'clock on my watch," she said. China had moved the hands back one hour; she leaned back on the bench and smiled at the tormented man. "Were you in a hurry to get somewhere?"

"Well, two o'clock," he muttered and looked around for confirmation of the time. "My watch is ten minutes fast, then."

"Where did you get that hat?" asked Angel. She complained about the heat from at least a block behind her husband. She had brushed her cheeks with a second coat of cosmetics.

"Remember that old woman on the platform?"

"No, you ran her down and stole it!" shouted Angel.

"Good for you!" shouted Cinch.

"No, no, she gave it to me," said China.

"Gave it to you?"

"Never!"

"Yes, she gave it to me."

"What for?"

"Well, she fell in the river and I pulled her out when no one else would help," related China. "We talked, she showed me her bound feet, and then she gave me the cap. Do you like the star?"

"Bullshit," snapped Cinch.

"These people never help each other," carped Angel.

"Come on, China, you either stole it or you found it on the bench," insisted Cinch. "Anyway, you look like a typical Mao mocker in a cap like that, with a Commie star no less."

"She gave me this little box of herbs too," said China. She opened the round metal box and raised the thick brown flecks close to his nose. The cover was decorated with bound lilies and pale monarchial portraits.

"What is it?"

"Some kind of herb," she said. China spread the contents on the palm of her hand. "The old woman showed me how to sniff it, open the nostils wide and inhale in short breaths, but the herb smells rather musty to me."

"Those are not herbs," he shouted. Cinch pinched his nose closed and moved back behind the bench. "Keep that shit away from me."

"Don't tell me."

"What is it then?" asked Angel.

"Scabs."

"Sore scabs?"

"You have a sick sense of humor," said China.

"Diseased scabs."

"Spare me, please."

"No shit China."

"Cinch knows, believe me," pleaded Angel.

"Rich Chinese picked smallpox wounds," he explained from the other side of the bench, "and shared the scabs with relatives, sort of a token inoculation, a smell for good health."

China returned the scabs to the metal box; her nose creased and her muscles trembled. "Nice box," she said and pinched the cover closed. She placed the box on the bench and wiped her moist hands on her trousers.

"Box, box, where is our box?" shouted Angel.

"Shit, did you lose our juice extractor?"

"Was that a juicer?"

"What did you do with it? Where is it" Angel shouted and pranced on the hard earth behind the bench. She pounded her arms, and her neck blushed with anger.

"Forgive me, when I rushed down the steps to help the old woman I left the box behind," explained China. "A juicer, no wonder it was so heavy."

"Where did you leave it?"

"Cinch, you told me that China is not a nation of thieves," chanted China. "Unlike America, you said, people always return things here, so what's there to worry about?"

"Nice move, now where did you leave the juicer?"

"Down three tiers," said China.

"What time is it Angel?"

"Two-fifteen," she answered, "but I thought it was later than that? What was the big rush then?" Angel leaned back on the wooden bench and sighed. "Our marriage has been a timed event; we are ruled by the clock."

"There, the box is down one tier, right where I left it," said China. More than a dozen men circled the carton with their hands behind their backs to read the news stories about the condemned criminals. What was in the carton did not seem to interest them.

"Are you really an Indian?" asked Angel.

"Not really," mocked China, "you see, my grandfather was a nobleman, he was the Baron of Patronia, and we inherited the baronage."

"Really?"

"Yes, really."

"The Chinese love titles; you got it made China," she said. Angel turned and watched her husband climb the stepped bank with their juice extractor.

"Angel, please don't wrap our packages with newspapers next time," he said, winded. Cinch unwrapped the carton. "These people seldom steal, but they read anything, even instructions."

"In that case," said China, "you should cover everything you own with newspapers. Consider it insurance, crowd protection of the contents."

"China is a lord, did you know that?"

"Of course," said Cinch.

"Listen, how did you know that?"

"She travels lighter than the rest of us."

"That's my Cinch," said Angel.

"We got nothing to lose, so wrap the other packages with newspapers, but turn those capital punishment stories under this time." Cinch leaned back on the bench; he wiped his beard and watched the boats on the river. "China," he sighed, "who would name a child China?"

CHINA and the WARRIOR CLOWN

China Browne trailed a horse cart from the Tianjin Hotel on Victoria Park to Zhou Enlai University. She waited outside the campus gate, a writer at the scratch line, with an invitation to interview a warrior clown about Griever. de Hocus, the trickster teacher from the baronage who had liberated hundreds of chickens at a local street market and then vanished last summer on a Patronia Microlight, an airplane built by Slyboots Browne on the White Earth Reservation.

China folded her arms beneath her breasts and lowered her head to duck a cloud of dust; the street sweepers, two women with white cotton masks, wheeled their brooms down the road as close as they could come to foreigners.

Wu Chou, the gatekeeper and warrior clown, waited for the dust to clear and then he waved the mixed-blood writer over the line and into the small brick house near the gatepost. China prepared to meet the clown; she brushed her hair, patted her blouse, and with a tissue, daubed her teeth, nose, and cheeks.

"China lovers strain at the windows like flies," he said and circled the low backless chairs until she seemed comfortable with his dramatic gestures. "Missionaries, tourists, and teachers, praise the obvious, our steam locomotives, plastic shoes, blue coats, red stars, and underwear, so much pathos in their clever trinities."

Wu Chou studied China as he circled the chairs: the slant of her shoulders, the round wrinkles on her elbows, the curve of her neck, her ears, the prominence of her nose, and her small hands spread like moist leaves over a miniature tape recorder. She wore white cotton trousers and a pleated blouse with blue sailboats printed in broken rows over her low breasts. Her head seemed to rise with a common pleasance, but her fingernails were trimmed too close, and when she smiled a thin scar creased the right side of her wide brown forehead. He smiled and pinched the humid air near her face, around her dark hair.

China has three unrivaled worries, and two obsessions. She is enchanted with the wild energies of smaller men, and she is fascinated with pictures of bound feet. As a child she bound her feet and earned her given name; she folded a blue bandanna, the same one that she wound on the toes of the old woman at the river, around her imperial toes and moved at night on ceremonial lilies from the baronage to other exotic places in the world. Once or twice a week, when she is lonesome, she draws silk ribbons between her toes, an unusual method of meditation.

"Most flies bounce on both sides of the pane, but tricksters are a mismatch at windows," he said. "Griever de Hocus, he was a dream liberator." Wu Chou tapped the brazier and watched the scar appear and disappear on her forehead.

China worries about demons in the blood, insects near her ears, and those moments when she loses connections with tribal time. She is worried that she could be suspended without a natural season, severed from her memories; these fears have delivered her to the sweet whims of clowns, the isocracies of tricksters, and blue bandannas.

"Griever was holosexual like most trickster clowns," said the warrior clown. He leaned closer and spoke into her hand, the hand that held the miniature microphone.

"Griever, gay?"

"Holosexual, not homosexual," he emphasized. "Griever, you see, he was the cock of the walk, he loved the whole wide world, and he told his students how much he loved you, too."

"He never said that."

"Griever said he loved you on that reservation mount, that warm place where it never snows and where no mosquitos enter. He told me that," said the clown.

"Did he reveal the mount?"

"Yes, and the Stations of the Cross."

"Positions of the trickster, he must have said something about his positions," she said and tapped her shoes together.

"He overturned our manners too, but he freed birds and never, never picked flowers, he became our mind monkey, you can write about that." Wu Chou paused to pinch the air around her knees. "But the world gave him too much trouble for his tribal time." He pitched his head forward, smiled, and placed a small kettle of water on the brazier. "The colonial world, you see, is tragic, but tricksters and clowns are comic, and that is the seam that a mind monkey mends."

"Mind monkey?"

"Yes, a holosexual mind monkey," he said and cocked his head to explain. "Griever loved women, heart gossip, stones, trees, and he collected lost shoes, broken wheels, the comedies of the lonesome and the lost."

"Griever learned how to collect lost shoes from his cousin Mouse Proof Martin who came to live with us on the baronage, and Mouse Proof's sister Wink married my father, Shadow Box," she chanted in rapid speech. "Griever was our trickster uncle, the uncle with the wicked hands, so we gave him that nickname."

"Wicked Hands?"

"Yes," she sighed.

"Wicked Hands de Hocus named his cock Matteo Ricci when he liberated the chickens at the free market," said the clown. "He marched down to the market and paid cash for one cock and more than a dozen caged hens, but he never told me about his wicked hands on the reservation."

"What did he do with them?"

"Matteo Ricci was last seen in flight with the trickster on his microlight airplane," the clown laughed. "Griever shooed the other hens down the market when the cutthroat flashed his knife over the blood-soaked counter."

"No blood, please."

"People were drawn to the trickster and his wild act, not to the high cost of chicken parts," he continued. "Mind monkeys, in our traditional stories, would have done no less than emancipate the birds at a free market. Those who liberate, even in a comic opera, are the heroes in our culture."

Wu Chou hunched his shoulders and turned his head to the side, a simian elocution pose from a comic opera scene. He raised his hands, wrinkled his nose, and pinched the smoke in the air around her shoulders.

"Holosexual indeed," she said and brushed her hair.

"Griever was the first foreign teacher to arrive that summer," said the clown. "He endured the air pollution, the bad water, the roar of cicadas, and the crowds, but not the Foreign Affairs Bureau."

The warrior clown crouched to fan the fire in the

brazier. He poured two bowls of black tea, smiled wide, and turned his head from side to side until she noticed two miniature butterflies on the loose wrinkled skin below his ears; he wore an opera coat with butterflies embroidered on the wide lapels. She laughed and applauded the docile dance of the insects.

The brick house was shrouded under deep sculptured eaves. The room was bare with three backless chairs around the brazier, a polished leather holster, and a metal box on a narrow counter over a window. The wide wooden door had been removed and then burned during the first winter of the revolution, the same winter that sewer covers were smelted on the campus and hundreds of people dropped through the holes at night.

Crickets held the four points of the room, and spiders molded the stained corners of the ceiling. Green katydids paused at the threshold in their season but never entered the humid room.

China watched his hands move in the smoke.

The warrior clown, a master of theatrical gestures, pinched the sun from his summer memories, over his maw and dark crotch, under faded tattoos; and he collected uncommon names from the last revolution.

"Griever was a dream liberator when our dreams had retreated like insects to the corners," he announced with one finger on his ear. "We remember our past in lost letters and colonial maps, the remains of the foreign concessions."

"The comic remains," whispered China.

"Look around at the architecture, the banks and hotels, the old names have disappeared, but we bear the same missions in our memories." He laughed and unsettled the butterflies under his ears. "Griever was our mind monkey."

China turned slantwise on the narrow wooden

chair, shifted from one cheek to the other, and brushed the dust from her white shoes. She listened to the clown and remembered the trickster with his wicked hands on women.

"We surrendered to the first missionaries," he said and then paused to hail a government official who was chauffeured through the gate in a black limousine. "We were students at the Nankai Middle School with Zhou Enlai, but now we speak a rather formal and footsore language."

"Premier Zhou Enlai?"

"Indeed, and we practiced new words on the run," said the clown. "We followed visitors to the parks and picked on their best euphemisms and colonial metaphors, and we even dared to pursue unusual phrases into forbidden restaurants, this, in our own nation, but the revolution turned out the old colonists and invited in the new capitalists."

Wu Chou supped from a bowl; steam rose from the hot tea and fogged the small round spectacles high on his nose. "But now we talk back on hard chairs and wait to translate the new verbs from trick menus."

"Was the trickster a good teacher?"

"Griever was wild on campus, but he was his best outside the classroom," said the clown. "He visited Victoria Park across from the Tianjin Hotel several times a week, and when he was approached by students who wanted to practice English, he taught them obscene words, the language of lust and sex."

"No wonder he vanished," said China.

"Mind monkeys can be dangerous," he said, "but liberation has never been explained with manners, we learned manners in the colonial concessions when ironies and comic lust would have been a more humane catechism to survive in the modern world."

Wu Chou, which means "warrior clown," a name he

earned from the classical theater, was an actor before the revolution. He is remembered for his brilliant performances as the Monkey King in the opera *Havoc of Heaven*. When he was too old to tumble as an acrobat, he studied the stories of tricksters and shamans in several countries around the world. He returned home to teach after the revolution and was banished to a political prison farm where he attended to chickens. A decade later, past retirement and keen on common fowl, his reputation as a scholar and warrior clown was restored; he accepted a simple sinecure as the overseer of the electronic portal at the main entrance to Zhou Enlai University.

"Griever came back from the street market that first morning whistling 'The Stars and Stripes Forever' with blood and feathers on his shoes," he said as he pushed the button to open the gate. A tired peasant and his disabled daughter saluted the winsome warrior from their horse cart loaded with platform poles.

"What on earth happened?"

"Griever freed the chickens and the cock spilled the blood on the counter," he said and held his mouth open. "He became the master of chicken souls, and Matteo Ricci, stained with blood, followed him back to the campus and up to his apartment in the guest house."

"Not blood, no more blood," she pleaded.

"Griever was our mind monkey, remember that, he was a real holosexual clown in his own parade," said the warrior clown with a wide smile. His teeth were uneven, stained with black tea.

"But tell me, was he ever evil?"

"Never evil, never, never," the clown chanted at the rim of the tea bowl. "Cocks never follow devils, cocks chase devils. Matteo Ricci followed the trickster and chased the other teachers in the guest house."

China was insecure, she crossed her arms and twisted one foot behind the other. She rocked from side to side on the chair and looked out the wide door toward the gate. The new trees were restrained at the wall, unnatural in the dust and charcoal smoke.

Wu Chou reached for a small metal box near the leather holster on the counter over the window. He dusted the box, opened it with care, and then he sorted through the contents, several dozen photographs.

"Look at this one," he said, as he moved behind the writer. He leaned over her right shoulder and presented the photograph with one hand close to her breasts.

"The same suede saddle shoes, he loved those shoes and those pleated trousers, he wore them on the reservation," she said and pointed at the color print. She held the photograph closer and studied the trickster.

"Griever was a natural clown," said Wu Chou. "See, we painted his face white, with red and gold, like a Monkey King for the Marxmass Carnival."

"Marxmass Carnival?"

"Father Omax Parasimo founded the celebration," the clown explained. "He was an unfrocked priest who taught architecture here, and he said it was a secular crotch where class wars and solemn communions contend, a natural endeavor in diacritical amusements."

"What was that again?"

"Secular abusements."

"Griever started that at the baronage," she said and touched her ear. "He called it 'harmless abusement' or 'the bald park where old men masturbate.' "

"Griever marked the observance here on the same night that we celebrate the autumn moon festival, or when the moon is bald and men beat the pond," said the clown.

Griever stood on one foot near the gatepost with a

bamboo pole raised over his head. He wore a bright lemon raglan coat and loose blue trousers. His face was blurred in each print, but the trees, strangers at the gate, even the old warrior clown, appeared in sharp focus.

"What's this here, in this print?"

"Horsehair duster."

"No, no, not the opera duster."

"What then?"

"This, he never wore a sporran on the reservation," she said and pointed with her little finger. She wore a beaded bracelet, the same color as the veins on her hands.

"Griever wore a holster," the clown responded as he leaned closer to her shoulder again, so close that she could smell garlic and feel his warm breath; his cheek touched her dark hair. He told her stories about the holster and watched the rise of her breasts, warm and brown, over the blue sailboats. When his small rough hand brushed the bare back of her neck, she shivered and returned the photographs.

China stopped the recorder and moved to the door, where she stood in the frame with her hands behind her neck. Her shadow coasted over the concrete, over the chairs, and folded like a child on the back wall. The warrior clown turned in the charcoal smoke and pinched a trace of her brown breasts from the floor. When she moved within the frame, her shadow broke from his reach.

"Why would he need a holster?"

"To shoot clocks."

"The chickens?"

"Clocks, clocks, ticktock, he loved cocks, he was a cock trickster, but he hated clocks," the clown said in a loud voice. "He carried a holster to shoot time, dead time on the clock."

"Clocks, of course, but did he tell you the stories about the tribal trickster who lived in a town clock and turned time back a few hours to calm the nerves of the people who were late?"

"No, never heard that one."

"What were his stories about, then?"

"Catholics."

"Griever told stories about Catholics?"

"Catholics on the White Earth Reservation," said the clown with his hands folded on his chest. "We remember the stories about the fourteen nuns at the mission."

"What nuns?"

"Order of Saint Rapacious," said the clown.

"Wait a minute," pleaded China.

"The Rapacious sisters lived in the wilderness, each one lived under a birch, and the trees were Stations of the Cross," he said. "His students remember the wild stations."

"Positions, no doubt," hooted China.

"You know these sisters?"

"Some, and the variations," she said at the door.

"The sisters raised their children under the birch, and he said the children became moveable stations on the reservation." Wu Chou circled the chairs and made animal shadows with his hands.

"This is crazy."

"The shadow creatures?"

"No, not that."

"Moveable Stations of the Cross?"

"No, no," she moaned, "but that you, a gatekeeper in the middle of China, are telling me stories about our reservation on the other side of the earth."

"My name is America," he mocked.

"But the stories are great, the trickster with the wicked hands and a broken zipper," she mumbled. "Tell me more about these children and their Stations of the Cross."

"The children were shadows, fourteen birch shadows, and they followed wicked parishioners into compromising situations and then diverted them," he said and raised his eyebrows. "The shadow stations were like a con-

"Clocks, of course, but did he tell you the stories fessional in advance, but the children became mind monkeys not saints, and these were the stories that brought the tribal trickster and the mind monkey together."

"Griever, the woodland mind monkey."

"Those people who dread the trickster and the mind monkey must dread their own freedom," said the warrior clown.

"But some people would rather not be tricked into their liberation," said China. She mumbled the last word, uncertain that she wanted to disagree. "Tricks are not ideologies."

"Mind monkey in a lost shoe?"

"Listen, when we heard that Griever was flying across China in a Patronia Microlight, the airplane my brother Slyboots built, my father was so impressed that he claimed him as a son and named him an heir to the baronage, which makes your mind monkey our trickster lord."

"Do you know where he has gone?" he asked.

"Macao?"

"No one knows. He started out for there, but he might have turned back to the Jade Gate at Dunhuang, back over the silk roads with the bear shamans, back to the golden ruins, the peaches and lapis lazuli, in the the ancient cities on the rim of the deserts."

"Griever never like the past or the desert."

"Macao, then," said the warrior clown. "Griever and Matteo Ricci in Macao." Wu Chou smiled, moved the butterflies under his ears, and saluted the trickster liberator from the wild threshold of the gatehouse.

Tune Browne

GRADUATION
with ISHI

Tune Browne has never been a celebrant; he never learned to croon, and he has never been invited to the blessed helm with the missionaries. The trickster roved near the border with mongrels under an enormous tricorne hat; he saluted the museum overseers, mounted the seasons down to the wild sea, overturned weathered barriers and minimal names in a comic parade.

Tune never wore beads or feathers or a wristwatch; he never paid much attention to time or to his wild images until one winter when he dressed in thin leathers and became an independent candidate for alderman in the cities. He never minded clocks or function words, no one expected him to win, but reporters listened to his unusual metaphors and presented his outsized nose on television. He improved his poses on late-night shows; he cocked his cheekbones higher to hold the bright light, to mimic old western photographs.

Bale De Moralia, his mixedblood manager, bought him a gold watch; the trickster held his breath and dressed in beads, bone bits, and furs. Later, on election eve, he appeared at parties, transformed in braids and ribbons, a proud invention and the reversal of the tribal striptease.

De Moralia argued that tribal cultures were colonized in a reversal of the striptease, and "now the trickster must remove his mock vestments in accordance with old photographs like those taken by Edward Curtis." Bale pointed out that Roland Barthes, the semiological adventurer, shows that the striptease is a wild contradiction; at that final moment of nakedness a "woman is desexualized."

Barthes writes in his book *Mythologies* that the spectacle is based on the "pretence of fear, as if eroticism here went no further than a sort of delicious terror, whose ritual signs have only to be announced to evoke at once the idea of sex and its conjuration." Familiar tribal images are patches on this "pretence of fear" and there is a sense of "delicious terror" in the structural opposition of savagism and civilization found in the cinema and in the literature of romantic captivities. Plains tepees, and the signs of mocassins, canoes, arrowheads, and numerous museum teasers, conjure the cultural rituals of the invented past; the pleasures of the tribal striptease are denied, data-bound in instrumental research, stopped in emulsion, colonized in written languages to resolve the insecurities and inhibitions of the dominant material culture.

De Moralia lectured that winter that the "striptease was primal, the first thrust in socioacupuncture, suspense account remedies that must be realized in festive time tricks, mythic verism, and tribal satire." He rails that "these eternal contradictions release the delicious ritual terror in captured images, so watch this wild candidate undress the invention and lose the election."

"Ishi never won an election, either," the trickster pleaded at the first international conference on socio-acupuncture and tribal identities. "He lived alone with one name, loose change, and a business suit in a corner of an institution, the captured candidate and the finished tribal ornament. The anthropologists who rescued him declared that his private seasons were their public ventures.

"Ishi the survivor, the last of his tribe, was collared in a minimalist diorama, an honored savage in a white world until he danced with tricksters in a tribal striptease at the University of California."

Tune posed on stage, the lead speaker on tribal identities in the modern world, between two photographic images. On the right side was his captured image in braids, sitting on the ground in a crowded tepee with several peace pipes and an alarm clock. The photograph projected on the left side of the screen was *In a Piegan Lodge* by Edward Curtis.

"See here," said the trickster as he pointed to the images, "Curtis has removed the clock, colonized our cultures, and denied us our time in the world.

"Curtis paid us for the poses," he said and stepped into his own image on the screen. "It was hot then, but he wanted us to wear leathers to create the appearance of a traditional scene, his idea of the tribal past. Curtis stood alone behind his camera, so alone, and we pitied him there because he seemed so lost, separated from his shadow, a desperate man who paid tribal people to become the images in his captured families. We never saw the photographs then and never thought it would make a difference, but we were consumed in camera time, we lost the election and became prisoners in his negatives."

Tune pushed the podium aside, raised his hands, spread his stout fingers, an avian salute, and released several feathers from his vest. The lights in the campus auditorium were dim; the audience was silent. The paper birch whispered in the back rows. Crows called in the distance, an otter slid down a riverbank and snapped back in mythic time as a trickster on a high wire between the woodland and the cities.

"Socioacupuncture is our means of survival on the wire, our striptease in mythic satire," the trickster said as he untied the ties of the mock vestments captured in photographs, unhooked the hooks to museum commodities, and bead over bead performed a slow striptease, a ritual contradiction between two projected images from the time-bound past. "This is not satire as shame, not social ridicule as a form of social control," he shouted as he dropped a bone choker to the floor, "but satire in magical connections with the oral tradition, mythic satire, not as a moral lesson, but a dream voice out of time like this striptease in the middle of the white word wars."

Tune removed his beaded leather vest, untied wing bones, and turned a sash; he danced and continued his stories on the ethos of the ritual striptease.

"Socioacupuncture reverses the instrumental documents, cold data is deflated, historical time is dissolved, and the pale inventors and consumers of tribal cultures are exposed when the pressure in captured images is released." The trickster untied his mocassins.

"Take it off," a woman shouted from the audience.

"Give him time," a man responded.

"Roy Wagner turned the peace medals and stopped the clocks when he wrote *The Invention of Culture*," said the trickster as he kicked his pinched mocassins with the floral bead patterns to the audience. "He wrote that 'the study of culture is in fact our culture,' the dominant white culture is what he means here, and 'it operates through our forms, creates in our terms, borrows our words and concepts for its meanings, and re-creates us through our efforts. . . . By applying universal theories naively to the study of culture we invent those cultures as stubborn and inviolable individualities. Each failure motivates a greater collectivizing effort.'

"We lose the elections in leather and feathers, failed and fixed in past histories, but through mythic satire we reverse the inventions, and during our ritual striptease the inventors and consumers vanish."

"Take it off," the audience chanted.

"Delicious terror," the trickster said as he unbuttoned his shirt and unbraided his hair and shivered between the captured images on the screen at his sides.

"More, more, more."

"Wagner tells how Ishi, the last survivor of the Yahi tribe in California, 'brought the world into the museum,' where he lived and worked after our capture," Tune confessed as he threw his shirt and the ribbons from his braids to the audience. "In good weather anthropologists would take the two of us from the museum back to the hills where we would demonstrate how to survive with a small bow and wooden arrows. He was the 'ideal museum specimen.
. . . Ishi accomplished the metaphorization of life into culture that defines much of anthropological understanding,' Wagner wrote."

"Take it off."
"Take it off."
"Take it off."
"Take it off."

"Tune is the captured name at the end of the culture games," he chanted as he combed his hair free from braids, and then he untied the beaded belt that held his leather trousers erect, "the end of the invented culture games." The inventors, missionaries, and the new research colonialists disappeared with the striptease, even those whose ideas he had quoted vanished like petals on a pasture rose. The conference on socioacupuncture turned silent once more.

Tune dissolved the scenes on the screen and stood alone in an undecorated breechcloth. He moved closer to the audience and told about the dour anthropologists who stole their stories. "But even so we received honorary degrees in the oral tradition from the University of California at Berkeley."

The graduation ceremonies were held in the redwoods, in the wild hills above the campus. Tribal ghosts hovered over the outdoor amphitheater in the Mather Redwood Grove. Birds soared in the treescapes, bears browsed on the mountains. Tune waved his hands and remembered the great flood, the tribal provenance, and called the crows back from the cities.

Alfred Kroeber, Thomas Waterman, Edward Sapir the linguist, and Phoebe Apperson Hearst, regent of the University of California, and past Presidents Robert Sproul and Benjamin Ide Wheeler were all there for the graduation ceremonies with the tribes, roundabout in the redwood trees, soaring out of time and place in magical flight.

"The University of California strives never to isolate academic ideas, races, or nations on our campus as single population groups. This is not a place of racial separations," asserted the provost as he pinched the loose skin under his wicked chin. "Our academic communities are based on trust, research, instruction, fair examinations and, of course, on excellence."

"Knock it off," three tribal women carped from the back rim of the amphitheater, "this one is our time not yours mister white man."

"Take it off," someone shouted.

"This afternoon we are privileged to announce that our very own Ishi and Tune Browne will receive honorary Doctor of Philosophy degrees here, at the University of California, where these two instinctive native scholars have lived. It is a distinct pleasure to announce these degrees and to introduce Alfred Kroeber, the famous anthropologist who worked with these two proud and unusual natives."

Kroeber was a gentle man; he shuffled to the stage, pulled the microphone down, leaned closer and, in a distant voice, told the audience that Ishi was the "most patient man I ever knew. I mean he had mastered the philosophy of patience. . . . "

Saxton Pope, the medical doctor and master of bows and arrows, was not present for the graduation, but he wrote the following to be read at the ceremonies in the redwoods: Ishi "looked upon us as sophisticated children—smart, but not wise. We knew many things, and much that was false. He knew nature, which is always true. . . . His soul was that of a child, his mind that of a philosopher."

Phoebe Apperson Hearst came down to the microphone from the right rim of the amphitheater to decorate Ishi and Tune Browne with colorful sashes and to present their degrees. "Doctor Ishi Ishi, Doctor Tune Browne Browne, you are both intuitive scholars, we have all agreed, may the Great Spirit hold your hands at the end. Doctor Kroeber has recorded the first words that Ishi spoke in English when he arrived at the museum, and we are at last pleased to imitate this fine man on this auspicious occasion; he said, is 'evelybody hoppy?' "

"The transvaluation of roles that turns the despised and oppressed into symbols of salvation and rebirth is nothing new in the history of human culture," writes Robert Bellah, a sociologist at the University of California, in his book *The Broken Covenant*, "but when it occurs, it is an indication of new cultural directions, perhaps of a deep cultural revolution." The trickster turned toward the anthropologists, "So remember that," he said and repeated the last phrase.

Tune and Ishi paraded down the aisles in the amphitheater, dressed in their breechcloths and academic sashes with animals and tribal spirits under the redwood trees. The two graduates circled the dais and then rendered a ritual striptease deep in a cultural revolution.

"Evelybody hoppy?" asked Doctor Ishi.

"What delicious terrors," said Doctor Tune Browne.

"Strip the anthropologists."

"Strip their words," someone shouted.

"Evelybody strip," three tribal women mocked from the back of the amphitheater, "that would make us very hoppy." The women unbuttoned their blouses and trousers as they moved down the aisle.

"Evelybody hoppy?" asked Doctor Ishi.

"Evelybody hoppy," mocked the trickster.

NEW SCHOOL of SOCIOACUPUNCTURE

Tune Browne packed his van last winter and moved to Berkeley where he established the New School of Socioacupuncture under his hat on Sproul Plaza at the University of California.

The "old school" was founded on a tragic worldview, the old domination watch, an invitation to territorial wars where both sides lose; the meed was material and the consumers were those loathsome plunderers of interior landscapes.

The New School of Socioacupuncture, aroused under colonial psalms on the reservation and nurtured in wild panic holes on the baronage, is an active word war with a comic temper; no one wins or loses in tribal comedies. The trickster argues that agonistic imagination comes with the oral tradition; chance, whimsical contention, dreams, and mythic verities bear the cold winters in the birch and the white nights in institutions.

Tune rears comic crows, bears, and shamans in his stories and poses; his tribal tread is continuous and he never holds time down to the ticktock on the clock. "The present is a wild season not a ruse," he said. "The trickster who would be a tree is not a lighthouse, and the shaman who bears leaves does not appear in photographs to measure his memories." The trickster salutes chance at common intersections, and at the seams between written words; he never answers riddles or those who ask the time on the clock. "Tricksters and trees pose with no leaves in winter."

The trickster is a comic liberator in the new word wars. He maddens culture cultists, erudite anthropologists, and quickens their leaden dioramas at the same time; he enlivens their dead letters and blackboard schemes. Last week, however, his comedies were blunted behind the law school.

White Lies remained at the wheel, true to the core, when a campus policeman ordered a tow truck to remove the patchwork mobile homestead with the reservation license plate. The van was worth much more impounded than double-parked, so the trickster retired his baronial license and rented a room.

Tune pursues culture cultists on the campus in the morning; in the afternoon the trickster is stationed under an enormous scarlet tricorne, where he bares the main pressure meridians in socioacupuncture and where he lectures on panic holes and how to hold back the clocks.

At dusk, when the cold ocean winds reach the campus, the trickster folds his tricorne, honorary degree, music stand, and returns, with White Lies, to his closet over the High Court, a vegetarian restaurant and liberation theology bookstore one block south of the campus on Telegraph Avenue.

One morning the trickster waited outside the classroom with the mongrels and promised that the "mongrels would overturn the best academies." Tune warned that "archaeologists sack the dead. Beware that anthropologists steal tribal stories, reduce popular memories to academic bilge, mismeasure imagination, and pretend to hold tribal tricksters on cultural lunge lines."

Professor Alan Dundas, the ostentatious consumer of tribal stories, launched his lecture on the tribal earthdiver. "The evidence available from folklore scholarship suggests that there is remarkable stability in oral narratives," he droned to an eager audience in Dwinelle Hall. "Myths and tales re-collected from the same culture show considerable similarity in structural pattern and detail despite the fact that the myths and tales are from different informants who are separated by many generations."

White Lies bounced down one aisle to the podium and barked at the anthropologist; a mongrel chow and two terriers howled down the other aisle. "The idea of anal creation myths spurred by male pregnancy envy," he continued and pretended not to hear the mongrels, "is not tied to the dream origin of myth theory. That is not to say the dream theory is not entirely possible but only to affirm the independence of the two hypotheses." White Lies circled the anthropologist and barked at his crotch; more mongrels wheeled into the auditorium and howled down the aisles. The students laughed, several howled back at the mongrels. Dundas ended his lecture on double negatives and hollow hypotheses.

"That reminds me that some doubles mean the opposite," said the trickster on the plaza. "Once upon a time the most learned linguists in the world gathered to discuss double negatives and positives. One elder lectured that some cultures use double negatives to mean the positive, but he had never heard, in all the cultures and languages that he had studied, a double positive that means the negative," said the trickster. He smiled, raised his tricorne on the breeze, and continued. "Way in the back of the auditorium a graduate student shouted, 'Yeah, yeah,' and brought the academic house down right into the wild present."

"Nae, nae," pleaded the anthropologists.

"Yeah, yeah," shouted the blonde.

"The present is an urban panic hole," the trickster lectured under the brilliant sun. Tune and a handful of new tricksters gathered under the tricorne that afternoon on the plaza: Fermi, a docent at the campus art museum who collects barber chairs; Bicker, a computer repairer with a cash settlement from a medical malpractice suit; Ex, a man with crosses painted over polka dots on his sweat suit; Token White, a blonde with a bow and arrows; Eros, a short bald woman with an archaic smile; White Lies, and several other mongrels. "The present is a natural reservoir where tricksters learn to dive and swim the backstroke."

Tune paused under his scarlet tricorne when the bald woman, dressed in a black sari with thick silver wings, wailed as she circled a bronze bear, the campus emblem. Her wild voice bounced between the buildings, a desperate pitch, and aroused White Lies.

"They stole my Putsch," wailed Eros.

"Whose pooch?" asked Bicker.

"Putsch not pooch," she snapped and lowered her sari. She was bald, a genetic state, with one pinch of black hair on the back of her head.

"Clean cut," said the blonde who towered over the bald woman. Token White, the name she had earned at urban sun dance ceremonies, hunkered down to her polished head and teased the thin black braid. "What made you so short and bald?"

"Shit, man, why do you carry that dumb bow, answer me that?" She sneered and circled the bear; the blonde lost her balance.

"Whose pooch is stolen?" asked Fermi.

"Never mind, never mind," the bald woman screeched. She beat her wings and pounded her bare feet on the concrete. White Lies, aroused by the loud voices, bounced in search of a panic hole and then barked at the trunk of a stunted sycamore on the plaza.

"Putsch, she said, not pooch," the blonde explained. She raised her shoulders and thumbed a staccato on the string of her bow.

"Who stole your Putsch?" asked Tune.

"Those assholes in life sciences," cursed the bald woman. Her mouth laid open between sounds; her tongue pressed the wide spaces between her teeth. "They stole my dog for some horrible experiment."

"Who are you?" asked Token White.

"Marilyn," she shouted. "Marilyn Monroe and those nazi bastards stole my Putsch, did you hear me tell you that?"

"No, no, you're not a blonde," said Token White.

"Eros is my real name," she said with a wicked smile. "Son of Aphrodite, goddess of love, did you hear me tell you that?"

"No, no, you're a woman," said Bicker.

"Not quite," whispered Eros.

"Men torture animals," announced Ex. He listened to the stories and marched at the margins, down a row of bricks laid in the concrete. "Men are defective women, that much we know from their research." His blue sweat suit was marked with white crosses. He wore blue-tinted sunglasses and a havelock; and he claimed to be a primitive rationalist.

"What's with the crosses?" asked Tune. He raised his tricorne and brushed his hair back behind his ears. "Last week you wore polka dots."

"That was then, this is now, the polka dot was my image, it was the easiest pattern to make in jail on the way back from an acid trip," he explained in a loud voice and moved his hands to simulate his position on the flight deck of an aircraft carrier. "The first polka dot was a hole in the floor, the only way out of the drunk tank, so I centered on the hole and I got out."

"Now you're cross?" asked Fermi.

"No, an X chromosome," he said. "Women have two, men one, which makes men defective women." Ex marched down a row, turned about, and marched back on the bricks. White Lies barked at the white crosses on his black tennis shoes.

"That's me, that's me," shouted Eros.

"What?"

"Neither ex nor wye," she said and raised the silver wings on her shoulders and moved them in magical flight, "not enough exes to be a woman, and not a whole wye to masturbate."

"Clown chromosomes," said the trickster, as he

chalked two crosses on the brim of his tricorne. Ex hooted and clapped his hands.

White Lies barked and bounced in search of a panic hole on the plaza; he settled for the bronze bear. Eros sucked on licorice behind an archaic smile and told the others what had happened to her chow mongrel with the black tongue. Tune punched his nose with his thumb and counted crosses. Ex directed pilots to the deck on a rough sea. Token White fingered her bowstring. Fermi washed his hands in the plaza fountain and enumerated his barber chairs. Bicker bickered with Eros.

"Putsch was captured yesterday by some science goons and taken to prison in the life sciences building," Eros shouted and pounded her bare feet. White Lies crawled under her sari and licked her hard little toes.

"Defective man, the ultimate torturer." Ex marched on the margin and muttered, "Many, many students have lost their pets on the campus this week."

"The disappeared," said Token White.

"Find my Putsch."

"Free the mongrels, liberate the mongrels in life sciences," chanted Tune, "this is our mission in socioacupuncture, free the animals." He folded his honorary degree, cocked his tricorne, and marched on the red margin, a brick row down past the plaza. Ex pranced in the lead, Eros hobbled behind the mongrels, Bicker and Fermi wandered wide, and Token White slouched at the end of the line with her bow and arrows.

Tune chanted, Eros shouted, Ex muttered and wheezed on the deck, Fermi moaned, Bicker carped, and Token White whistled over the creek; the column marched behind the theater to the life sciences building. There were wild creatures snared in concrete over the south entrance and animal death masks decorated the laboratories.

Ex pinched his nose, the building smelled of alcohol and formaldehyde. The column marched in silence around each level and listened for the sound of animals; the tricksters did not ask for directions. Token White opened every door and searched in closets, private toilets, and laboratories. Eros hunted in the same rooms behind the blonde and sneezed in the dark.

White Lies raised his nose on the third level; he smelled the mongrels and barked in wild circles down to the end of the corridor. There, in a room crowded with metal cages, several scientists carried out their research on mongrels.

Eros rushed into the room, pounded her bare feet on the cold terrazzo, and demanded her mongrel. The scientists leaned over their chemicals and machines in silence; no one responded to the bald woman at the end of the white marble tables. She pounded the counter and turned to search the cages on the aisles.

Token White braced her short curved Apache bow, made from a white hickory wagon wheel hoop, drew a hazelwood arrow with trimmed woodpecker feathers and a hand flaked obsidian point, and aimed it at a blond man in a white coat. The scientist did not respond so she lowered her aim; the arrow shattered a plastic radio case. When the rock music stopped, the scientists noticed the tricksters.

"What is this, a medieval heist?"

"No, postmodern socioacupuncture."

"Who are you?"

"Pooh Bah the mongrel liberator."

"Try the next lab. We're not mikados."

"Putsch."

"You listen to Tune," warned Token White. She drew an arrow and waved her bow at the scientists, who had moved closer together at the end of the table.

"What tune?"

"Tune Browne, the Baron of Patronia."

"Postmodern, indeed," said the blond scientist.

"Call me Tune," said the trickster. He raised his tricorne, smiled, and bowed to the scientists. "We are here this afternoon to free the birds."

"Sorry, no birds here."

"To liberate the mongrels," the trickster shouted.

"This is not a comedy?"

"Yeah, yeah," said Fermi.

"You're serious?" asked a scientist.

"Putsch."

"This is comic, and we are serious," said Tune.

"Why an animal rights raid now?" one scientist pleaded. "We had this settled last week at a meeting in the campus club with the chancellor."

"No, this is mongrel liberation."

"Putsch."

"Mister Tune, listen, our research could save human lives," said the blond scientist. "You're a reasonable man, would you hold up a cancer cure?"

"Putsch."

"Free the mongrels," the trickster shouted, "and save these scientists from cancer and their wicked research." Tune threw open the cages and the mongrels licked his hands.

"Wait, wait."

"Putsch, talk to me, please talk to me," Eros pleaded to her chow mongrel. Putsch licked her bald head with his black tongue. She pleaded, but he had lost his bark. The mongrels were hoarse, none could bark because the scientists had severed their vocal cords.

"Cruel bastards," cursed Token White. She drew her bow and ordered the scientists down on their backs, hands behind their heads on the terrazzo, and then she sicked the mongrels on them. Putsch circled the scientists, but he would not touch them. White Lies raised his leg and pissed on the blond; the other male mongrels, in turn, declared their territories on the scientists.

"Nazi doctors, cut their barks out," screeched Eros.

"Defective men," said Ex. He turned the scientists over and marked their white coats with black crosses; then he marked their cheeks and brows.

Ex was praised with each cross; he turned the scientists over once more and then he removed their clothes and marked their white bodies with black crosses. "Women have two, men one," he chanted over their bodies, "scientists have none."

Eros raised her sari and invited White Lies to lick her toes while Putsch licked her bald head. "Marilyn Monroe never had it this good, even if she was a blonde."

Tune returned to the plaza and told stories under his hat about the clown chromosomes that crossed over into the life sciences. The liberated mongrels with no barks became the most honored breed at the University of California.

Tulip Browne

WINDMILLS and CRAZY PAPERS

Tulip Browne is obsessed with wind and natural power; she builds miniature windmills in her new condominium in the hills. She throws open the windows and listens to the ocean wind over the copper blades of seventeen windmills; at dawn she attends a palace of whirs and secret twitters.

Once a week she wanders on the lower streets to encounter poor and destitute people; to brush with contention and common pleasures. The rude misconnections, wild separations, and blame shouted on the streets remind her of natural power and her untamed relatives in woodland reservation dreams. "Those down and out people," she told her mother, "are overlooked thunder storms in the cities, and we need their storms and stories to remember we are alive."

Tulip reveals no secrets and she bears no confessions from the baronage or her mixedblood identities; her sensitive moves are secluded, but she haunts memories with her personal power. She invites street people to dinner at the best restaurants and challenges them to a "persona grata rencounter."

"Do you know what that means?"

"Listen," he sighed behind his shopping cart.

"What is your name?"

"No," he shouted and waved his arms. His wild voice aroused two white cats in a cardboard box lashed to the top of his cart.

"No what?"

"No I don't know what you mean," he said.

"How about dinner?"

"When?"

"Down the block at the Krakow on the Vistula."

"You name it, you got it, you pay it," he said and pushed his cart down the sidewalk at her side. He parked under a bright red canopy at the entrance to the restaurant and covered the white cats with a broken parasol. "This place never leaves any garbage out, did you know that?"

"Have you ever eaten here?"

"Persona grata, what does that mean?" he asked and folded a thick slice of black bread over three butter cones. He lowered his head and leaned closer to the table, an animal over bread and butter.

"Persona grata means one is acceptable and welcome," she said, "and rencounter means to meet, an unplanned meeting, that's what I'm doing with you."

"Chance, you mean?"

"Yes, you could put it that way."

"Ronin Bloom," he mumbled over his bread.

"What?"

"Ronin Bloom," he shouted, "that's my name, not my real name, but my name, persona nongrata in the uppity hills where you come from sister." He finished the sentence and the black bread at the same time.

"Sir, could you leave your rope outside," said the black waiter. His forehead wrinkled when he spoke; he pinched his nose. "The rope, man, the rope, out, out, now."

Ronin wore a blue leather necktie, a paisley shirt, an oversized matted wool coat, threadbare wide-ribbed corduroy trousers, black boots with no heels, and thick canvas knee pads. He had not violated the liberal dress code in the restaurant, but the rope and his pungent odor would have been enough to remove him with reasonable cause.

"The rope, man, now."

"My cart's on the end of this," he said with the rope in his hands. One end of the thin orange tether was tied to two shopping carts parked under the canopy, and the other end encircled his waist in the belt loops.

"Could he bring his carts inside?" asked Tulip. She cocked her head and folded her hands on the rim of the table.

"I'm afraid not."

"Give me one good reason."

"Well, the stench is enough," said the waiter, his hand over his nose. He moved back from the table and summoned the owner of the restaurant.

"The shopping carts block the entrance, which in case of fire is very dangerous, but that's not the real problem," said the stout owner in rapid speech. "The cats are in violation of the city health code."

Ronin pushed his chair back in preparation to defend the honor of his two shorthairs, but the chair was on rollers and the gesture was lost in a collision with another table. "Man,"he said to the owner, "I'm a streetwiser and nobody talks about my family like that, but nobody. Whistle and

Black Duck were born on my carts."

"Perish the thought," the owner smirked.

"The carts are their home and my place too, our place, the carts are a sovereign place, we got everything we need on eight wheels," he shouted at the owner.

Ronin moved around the restaurant, from table to table, and repeated his stories about his sovereign carts. The customers were overwhelmed and covered their noses with monogrammed napkins when he landed too close to their tables. One woman covered her head and whimpered. "Sure, you can sit there with your keys to a house in the hills. Well, this rope is my key, man," he said to the shrouded woman. "So, who's crazy around here, me and my rope or you under that dumb napkin?"

"Please, sir," said the owner.

"Ronin is my name."

"Mister Ronin, sir, would you please step outside with us now?" The owner and three waiters surrounded the streetwiser, pushed him down into a chair, and rolled him out of the restaurant. The owner tripped on the orange rope and cursed street people; he hated the destitute and even denied them garbage from the restaurant.

Tulip paid for the two meals; the owner delivered the food outside in decorative cartons embossed with an imperial seal and Krakow on the Vistula. The cartons were tied with cotton braids. She cocked her head and assured the owner that she would return soon, but her gestures were lost in the confusion. The owner and three waiters rushed to the back of the restaurant to block the streetwiser and his carts.

Ronin Bloom had pushed his tandem shopping carts through the restaurant and parked between two tables at the rear. There he presented his collection of lost shoes and told stories about Black Duck and Whistle to seven customers. The waiters rushed the streetwiser and pushed his carts out the back door onto the trash landing.

"Whistle does but Black Duck is white . . . listen, I've got my crazy papers, you can't treat me this way," were his last words when the owner cursed him once more and slammed the steel door closed.

Ronin and Tulip pushed the carts down the main street to a park bench between a hotel and a bank. He ate with his fingers from the embossed carton and repeated his best lost shoe stories.Tulip listened and fed the cats on a thick golden napkin.

"My uncle has a shoe collection," she said.

"So, what's his name?" he asked and wiped his mouth on his matted sleeve. He wiped his hands on the shorthairs.

"Mouse Proof Martin."

"Never heard of him," he mumbled.

"No one has a better lost shoe collection," she boasted. "He even travels around and shows his shoes at colleges and museums."

"Maybe so," he shouted over the roar of a diesel bus, "but no one has a better lost shoe collection in a shopping cart, you can believe that."

"What got you started?"

"Sylvan Goldman."

"Relative?"

"Better than that, he was a grocer," he sighed and teased the shorthairs on their tethers. "Goldman's invention changed the world."

"Plastic clothes?" she teased in response.

"Shit no, he invented the shopping cart, the nesting cart, my tandem wheels, my mobile home where the urban buffalo roam," he chanted and waved his hands.

"Nice tune. Still hungry?"

"No, that crack on the river place was too much," he said and then turned his hands over and over on his knees. "Street people eat faster than the uppity hill people, you know."

"Why do you wear knee pads?"

"Balance," he shouted.

"You mean weights?" she said and ducked his breath.

"No, no, you know," he hesitated, "like two gloves, same shoes, balance like that, balance on the run, because I only have to wear one."

"Tell me, which one?"

"Look at this knee," he said and raised his right trouser leg. He wore no socks and his ankles were marbled black. "See, the patella is gone, broken and removed. The doc said wear a pad or lose my leg, so, two pads for me, balance."

"Ronin, you have nice legs."

"No woman ever said that to me before," he mumbled and covered his knee. "You got nice legs too. Do you live in the hills or something?"

"Yes, with a mongrel."

"What's his name?"

"White Lies."

"Shit, is that a real name?"

"Reservation name."

"You heard about crazy papers?"

"No, but you said something about that back at the Krakow on the Vistula," she said. "Should I have crazy papers?"

"Definitely. With a dog named White Lies, you definitely need your own crazy papers," he said and laughed. His teeth were stained and marked with caries. "Did you ever take your hound to a black hangout and call his name?"

"Never."

"Then you need crazy papers," he said and stretched his hands. Ronin opened a blue folder and removed an official certificate. He touched a pencil stub to his tongue and asked, "So, what's your real name?"

"Tulip Browne."

"Twolips and White Lies," he repeated and printed it on the document. "Now, with this, you can hangdog the street, wander into restaurants and search for food, and stay out of jail because the cops will know you're a wacko lodge member and not a case from Club Mental."

"Do I get a cart with crazy papers?"

"You ever heard about Terry Wilson?" he asked and propped his boots on the back of the carts. Black Duck pawed the holes in his soles.

"Does he have crazy papers?"

"He wrote *The Cart That Changed the World: The Career of Sylvan Goldman*, and that book and the cart changed my world," he said. "Goldman invented the nest cart, and I declared the tandem cart a sovereign state on low wheels.

"Sylvan made a seven-minute movie about how to use his invention because men would not be seen behind a cart. Well," he said and scratched his ear, "my mother saw that movie when I was born and it changed our lives, she decided that the cart was a perfect baby nest. She was the first person to buy her own cart to keep me in. So here I am, over twice as many wheels now."

Ronin unloaded a down sleeping bag, pushed several bundles of soiled clothes aside, and revealed his library and personal files wrapped in black plastic at the bottom of one cart.

"Here's my mother with me and our first nest cart,"

he said and selected several other photographs from a cigar box. "This one was my first elevator ride in my cart, the sides were decorated with crepe paper."

"Wait a minute."

"What?"

"Who's that with the beaded belt buckle?" she asked. Tulip pointed to an enormous stomach at the side of the photograph.

"Rainbow, that's my uncle, he lived with us for a time," he said and turned the photograph to read the inscription on the back. "Mogul's Department Store, October 23, 1939, with Rainbow, the day he said we're going to Oklahoma."

"You traveled in your cart," she mocked.

"Right, on the train," he said and passed her several photographs of his mother and various new carts painted in bright colors. "Rainbow got a job at the Folding Carrier Corporation in Oklahoma City because Sylvan Goldman owned the company and he liked to hire Indians way back then."

"Where is his face?"

"Who?"

"Rainbow, nothing but his stomach here."

"Well, somehow, he never got his face into a picture," he said and sorted through a stack of irregular shaped photographs, "nothing but his gut, you're right, and that beaded belt, except this one where you can see his boots and the brim of his cowboy hat. He always wore that hat, even to bed."

"Rainbow with no head."

"Listen," he said as he closed the cigar box, "you're a really nice person, you can borrow my cart book to change your world too." The book was covered with plastic, an unmarked treasure. "This is the only book that really counts, the only one I ever read cover to cover."

"Ronin, do you like windmills?"

"You got a windmill book that changed your world?"

"I build miniature windmills."

"No shit, where?"

"Meet me here on this bench in one week," she said. Tulip leaned forward and buttoned her coat. "I'll return your book then and give you one of my windmills. You can mount it on the front of your cart."

"Whistle loves the wind."

"Next week then?"

"Tulip, what a name for a streetwiser, and she even makes little windmills," he shouted as she crossed the street.

"Who cares? I got my crazy papers right here," she shouted back and then disappeared behind a bus at the intersection.

TERROCIOUS and the DEAD HEAD

Tulip Browne opened the windows and listened to the ocean wind turn the blades on her windmills. She remembered a humid night on the blue meadow when she heard voices but no one was there.

White Lies raised his head and moaned when the telephone chimed over her memories. Tulip has two numbers, one personal, and the other as a private investigator; the business line has a recorded message. She touched the copper blades as she passed and answered the personal chime.

"The windmills whir down to the bone this morning," she said, certain that no one but relatives and close friends would call on her unlisted number.

"Sounds wild to me," said a male voice.

"Who is this?" she demanded.

"Terret Pan-Anna, listen . . . "

"How did you get this number?" she asked and then pressed a button to record the conversation. "Who are you, why are you calling me at home?"

"Tulip, is this Tulip Browne?"

"Answer me," she insisted.

"Tune, your brother, he gave it to me," he said with less humor. "He gave me your number, he said it was a secret and told me to eat the number. Anyway, when do you answer your machine?"

"Who are you?"

"Professor Pan-Anna," he announced, "chairman of the Native American Indian Mixedblood Studies Department at the University of California, but you can call me Terrocious."

"Terrocious?"

"Listen, we need your help to investigate a serious problem of witchcraft and a stolen computer here," he pleaded. "We can talk about the details later."

"Witchcraft?"

"Owl heads, dead heads, rattles, whistles, and crackpot shamans," he chanted, "have the faculty and students on edge of their seats. Will you meet me for lunch to at least talk about our problem?"

"Where?"

"You name it this time," he said with confidence.

"Krakow on the Vistula."

"Fantastic, tomorrow at noon then," he said. Later he called her business number, listened to her recorded voice several times, and then he dictated, "I promise to eat your personal number when we meet if you promise to answer my calls and tell me more about the windmills close to the bone."

"How much?" she asked and considered the menu.

"Lunch is on me," he said and smiled.

"No, not the lunch," she said and closed the menu. "I mean how much money do you have set aside to pay me as a private investigator?"

Pan-Anna explained that Professor Marbell Shiverman, the author of *Native Americana Feminine Folklorica* and other studies of shamanic stories, had received in the mail a dead owl head, but the university police were reluctant to investigate tribal religious practices as criminal activities. He construed that urban shamans had became more material and their stories more humorous. "But then," he whispered and leaned closer to the private investigator, "we lost a new computer and other equipment." Terrocious touched her arm and watched the goose pimples rise; but he did not understand, the papillae response was an aversion not an adduction.

"Why are you telling me this?"

"Simple," he sighed, "would you investigate?"

"Have you notified the police?"

"No, no," he said and then leaned closer. He whispered, "That's part of the problem, you see, we would like some solid evidence to take care of this ourselves. We're a new department and what we don't need now is bad publicity about our faculty to feed the racists."

"Two thousand dollars, minimum," she announced.

"What?" he shouted.

"My fee to investigate," she said and repeated the amount, "in consideration of what you have told me so far. You can be sure that not one dollar of that amount is based on idealism or racialism."

"You're right about that," he said and wiped his mouth. He pushed the plate of sour sausages aside and spread his fingers down on the table, a sign that he had reached the bottom line in the conversation. "We have only a thousand, but how do we know you'll provide the information we need to solve this problem?"

"Why did you call on me then?"

"You're right again," he mumbled and closed his hands.

"One thousand cash or your personal check in advance," she said and then mocked his hand movements. She spread her small hands down on the table.

"Tune never told me his sister was such a hard driver," he said and turned from side to side in the swivel chair. "His humor has been a real treasure on the campus, especially at our last graduation when he came down on the anthropologists."

"Tune spends too much time under his hat to suit me," she said and smiled, "but he's a real trickster. Listen now, here are my conditions . . . "

"Surprise me."

"First, my report will be in the oral tradition and told to you, no one else, in less than a week," she emphasized. "I will describe several scenes and imagined events as stories, but the interpretation and resolution of the information will be yours, not mine. There will be no written report unless the same information is given to the police at the same time. You must agree to these conditions."

"Why do I feel like I've just bought a special stretch of blue sky over a swamp," he said. Terrocious stared at her and then he laughed, but he was nervous and uncertain.

"Because you have, but the stretch is a baronage."

"Could we get personal for a minute?" he asked and turned in his chair. "Tell me about your windmills, what whirs close to the bone?"

"I build windmills," she said and sliced a meatball on her plate. "Miniature windmills to catch the wind, natural power."

"Catch me," he pleaded and spread his hands.

"Too much wind," she said and laughed.

"How did you become a private investigator? You must be the only mixedblood in the business, and from a reservation no less."

"Eat my personal number."

"That was a joke," he said and clapped his hands.

"Not to me."

"I don't have the number with me."

"Here, eat my business card then; your promise is recorded,"she said. Tulip wrote her personal number on the back of an embossed card.

Pan-Anna examined the folded card, then he cut out the number, soaked it in sour sauce, and ate it with a morsel of sausage. "You're a hard woman," he said and swallowed. He might have pouted as a child; that expression was marked on his forehead. He craved the attention of this woman.

"Now, tell me about your names," she said with her elbows on the table. When the black waiter cleared the dishes, he recognized her and wrinkled his brow. "Tell me, is your nickname an adjective like ferocious?"

"Terrocious was a short sentence in public school," he said, pleased to tell stories about himself. "When I was in high school the principal was so angry with me once that he combined the words terrible and atrocious when he cussed me out. Well, I made the mistake of telling that story at a faculty party and the name stuck, as you might have imagined."

"How about Pan-Anna?"

"Now that is an interesting story," he said and expanded his chest. He had gained some weight over his academic worries and the winter; his shirt buttons were strained. "But tell me about your name first."

"No, not now. Please continue."

"Pan-Anna goes back a long way, back to the Pan-American Exposition of 1901 in Buffalo, New York," he said and touched her bare arm and then her shoulder.

Tulip shivered and rubbed her arm. She is fascinated with natural power, wind and water, but she hates most tribal men, even mixedbloods when they assume a racial connection, an unnatural privilege based on pigmentation and tribal cultures. Blond women, she has observed, have become the new material possession and are treated better than tribal women. When she resists a tribal man, her features become haunted, an animal at the treeline. Tulip moved back from the table when his wild breath touched her hair.

"Better that my grandfather was inspired with the birth of Pan-Anna than the death of William McKinley at the Pan-American Exposition," he said and moved closer. "Can you imagine my name being Terrocious McKinley?

"My grandfather was part of the Indian Congress at the exposition, one of the human types in an ethnological village, but he never seemed to mind," he said and cleared his throat several times. "He loved it, he told us stories about walking around the Evolution of Man exhibit with Geronimo, and the time he met William Jennings Bryan, the lawyer and politician, that gentleman chimpanzee Essau, and my grandfather was there at the Temple of Music when

President McKinley was shot by the anarchist Leon Czolgosz.

"But what impressed him the most at the exposition was when Vice President Theodore Roosevelt named a tribal child, the first born at the concession," he said and raised his hands to enhance the suspense. "Roosevelt named that baby Pan-Anna, and my grandfather was so impressed with that exposition name that he adopted it as our surname."

"Did he consider Czolgosz?"

"No, not even the vice president, but my grandfather was touched in a most unusual way, a religious experience of sorts, with the birth of that child at the exposition," he said in a solemn tone. "That child was the beginning of something new for him, a new tribal time, a new culture, and a new name."

"Luster Browne, my grandfather, was a tribal baron," she said and moved closer to the table. Tulip opened one of her business cards and drew on the back a map of the White Earth Reservation. "Patronia, the name of his federal allotment, is right here, not far from the source of the great Mississippi River."

"Fantastic," he said and touched her shoulder.

"Shadow Box, my sweet father, gave us all nicknames, such as Tune, China, Ginseng, Slyboots, Mime, and Garlic, and mine was Tulipwood, because my skin was the color of tulip wood at birth," she said and looked around the restaurant. The owner and one black waiter watched her from a distance. "We are all wild heirs to that reservation baronage."

"Fantastic," he swooned.

"Mime was silent, the most beautiful person in our family," she whispered and folded her arms. "I loved her more than anyone. We were twins, and she was born with no palate, no voice, no spoken words. Mime learned the most honest gestures in language, and she brought us closer together with her silent play and imitations. She mocked me, but she knew our mother better than anyone, she moved her hands and winked just like our mother. Her face was radiant with humor, her eyes were a dance, she had no fear, she was at peace with the world, and it was her pure love and trust, her innocence and silence that brought her to a violent death."

Tulip leaned forward in silence. Her breath was short and sudden; she turned her head to one side. Her knuckles turned white when she folded her hands. The overhead fan churned the thick air in the restaurant. "Garlic was killed by lightning on the meadow and the next night my beautiful sister Mime was raped and murdered behind the old mission house."

"Tulip, no more now."

"Well, listen, that's how I became a private investigator,"she said and shivered. "I was nineteen then, home from college for the summer, and it took me more than a year of investigation to convict three white men and one mixedblood of rape and murder, four drunken bastards on a hunting trip, looking for a savage, but they hated what they found because she was pure, a silent voice that reminded them of their own savagism."

"Please, no more now," he pleaded and then covered her hands with his; he was gentle and warm. "This is when a trickster would resolve the moment with tribal stories, a wild turn in a cruel world."

Tulip waited for his personal check to clear before she started her investigation. She called each faculty member in the department and asked them about dead owls, shamanism, and the stolen computer; she recorded each conversation and studied the voice patterns on oscillographs.

Professor Marbell Shiverman was the last person

she called late that afternoon. Tulip asked her about owls and other dead heads; she was eager to discuss evil possession and moved the conversation with her own rhetorical questions.

"How many heads have you received?"

"One, an owl head, dead."

"Naturally."

"Cruel and unusual," said Shiverman.

"Do you have pets?"

"Moan, our lonesome black cat."

"Where did you receive the dead head?"

"Where?"

"I mean, at home?"

"No, the office."

"Who delivered the owl head?"

"The postman."

"Was the package postmarked?"

"Well, the owl head was in my box when I arrived at the university that morning," she said in a monotone, "but we never thought to keep the postmark."

"There was someone else there?"

"The secretaries."

"Did you keep the dead head as evidence?"

"We put it in the freezer."

"Who would send you an owl head?"

"Tulip, what a beautiful name, listen, let me put it this way," she said and then inhaled through her nose, a low whistle, "I am a gay feminist, need I say more?"

"Feminists mailed you a dead head?"

"Men, men, that's who," said Marbell Silverman.

"Why would a man send you a dead head?" she asked in a firm tone of voice. Tulip turned more pleasure on the wind, the wind over copper blades on her miniature windmills, than she ever did in bed with men; but even so, she would never crib her own real experiences with crude ideologies based on gender.

"Listen, the men in the department hate me, they have tried, believe me, to get rid of me because they refuse to accept gays or feminists," she said. The words were aggressive signifiers, but her voice was monotone, a cold heart on the oscillograph.

"Professor Pan-Anna has hired me to investigate the origin of the owl head and the loss of the computer," she said. "Do you know anything about what happened to the computer?"

"Nothing, why do you ask?" Her voice wavered and rose three tones on an octave. "Pan-Anna loaned the computer to a male friend of his, and now he's trying to blame me for it, but we know what he's up to this time, we know about his sexism."

"He told me he would rather have the computer returned, with no blame," she said with precision. "Pan-Anna told me he would rather avoid the university police and a stolen property report."

"That man is a liar, you can take my word for it," she said with a whistle and then paused. "Listen, once a week we have a tribal healing ceremony for women here at our home, why don't you come over and relieve your burdens?"

"Perhaps, next week then?"

"Pan-Anna is an evil man, and if you don't believe me then come over and you can hear for yourself what the women in the department have to say about him."

"No man is a saint, but evil is a cruel measure of human experience," she said and stopped the conversation. The voice patterns were smooth over the dead head conversation but peaked when the stolen computer was mentioned.

Tulip visited the department the next morning; she obtained an accurate description of the stolen computer, the weight and measurements of the carton, and estimated the distance from various offices to the loading dock behind the building. She examined scratch marks on the polished tile floor where the carton had been dragged in the main office. The marks ended at the door.

"Has the hallway been polished since the computer was stolen?" she asked. Tulip pointed at the marks and held her distance from the chairman.

"No, once a year in summer," he answered. "First it was my secretary and now you both seem obsessed with the marks on the floor. So what do the scratches tell you?"

"Nothing."

"Terrific, what else is new?"

"Marbell Shiverman said you were a sexist."

"Of course."

"That's what I said too."

"Wait a minute, whose side are you on?"

"Mine."

"I like a woman on her own side."

"Of course," said Tulip.

"Never mind the rest," he moaned.

"She said you and the other men in the department were trying to force her out because she is gay," she said. Tulip browsed in his office, examined his library and tribal artifacts. She read the introduction to a book on the woodland trickster.

"What did you tell her?"

"The truth," she said with a smile.

"But the truth is the problem."

"My intent is to tell her the truth, enough to make her nervous if she is guilty, and if she is nervous enough she might make a mistake and return the computer."

"Of course," said Terrocious.

"Now, where were you on the night of the crime?"

she asked and turned from the bookcase. Tulip sat down at the side of his desk and crossed her legs. She wore a loose cotton blouse with wide sleeves.

"In bed with a blonde," he boasted. Terrocious leaned back in his swivel chair and watched the dark space between her legs, under her short skirt.

"What kind of car does she drive?"

"The blonde?"

"Shiverman."

"Something small and foreign," he mumbled with marginal interest. "I can picture her corpulent arm pressed against the side window, and, come to think of it, she drives an old pink pickup too."

"Does she have a reserved parking place behind this building?" she asked and uncrossed her legs and turned in the chair.

"Yes," he sighed.

"Fantastic," she mocked and departed.

"Wait a minute," he shouted and followed her down the hall to the stairs. He watched her narrow thighs reel down the steps to the rear entrance of the building.

Terrocious told her there, on the loading dock, that a few days after the computer was stolen, "Shiverman reported to the police that her office, less than a hundred paces from this very spot, had been burgled. Her long list of stolen things was unbelievable, the owl head was first, followed by a cat litter box, an ash tray, and last but not least, an expensive electric typewriter that belonged to the department."

"She reported the owl head?"

"Not only that," he said with mock excitement, "but she reported that the official file on the investigation of the owl head was stolen."

"Too obvious."

"That's what the university police thought, accustomed as they are to peculiar professors," he said and moved closer. He brushed her right thigh. "Shiverman, however, was a real test of their imagination."

Tulip was admired as an honest private investigator; in eight years she had established confidential contacts in police agencies and most public services institutions. She obtained university police records that reported a pickup parked behind the building the morning after the computer was stolen; the report was a routine investigation because several pickups had been stolen that month. She obtained copies of service bills from Pacific Gas and Electric and reports on Marbell Shiverman's telephone charges in the past three months; she also located a computer store where supplies had been purchased for the same computer model that was stolen.

Terrocious hemmed and hawed on the telephone; he called several times to remind her that she had promised an oral report in less than a week. Tulip increased the volume of his recorded message and then opened the windows to listen. "Remember, never mind, but listen, would you like to get together, well, when your report is prepared in the oral tradition, or sooner, anytime, how about tonight? How about dinner?" he droned. He used most of the time on her recorder that week.

White Lies barked at his recorded voice.

Tulip agreed to meet him for lunch on the patio at the faculty club; there, on the campus, she would present her oral report over a tuna salad sandwich. She spread horseradish on the dark bread and told her stories about the owl head and the computer.

"Once upon a time there was a professor who could never remember the postmark on a package that contained an owl head, even though she said it was delivered to her mail box at the university," explained the trickster detective.

"This is hard to believe because the professor considers it to be so serious, and because she had invited secretaries and students down to her office to witness that dead heads had been delivered. The secretaries confirmed that she opened her mail, letters, and packages before she left the main departmental office."

"So, what does that mean?"

"She delivered her own owl head," she said and nibbled at her sandwich. "This professor is not an imaginative person, that much can be determined from her publications."

"The gay victim with a dead head," he mumbled and sliced a melon. "And men wear the black hats and owl masks in these wicked stories."

"She was so hated, one faculty member told me, that an owl head would never be enough, maybe a horse head, or a barrel of pig umbles," said Tulip. "But what are umbles?"

"Umbles, animal guts, like eating humble pie."

"That's what he meant?"

"What else?" said Terrocious.

"Her voice oscillograph crested on computers."

"You analyzed her voice?"

"The whole faculty."

"And me, describe my oscillograph then."

"The phallic mountains," said Tulip.

"Of course, what else can be raised by words?"

"She is more concerned about computers than owl heads, men, or even sexism, and that surprised me when she cursed men as evil," she said and turned toward the sun. "The professor has a monotone voice, expressionless at times, but she seems to attract extremes to break her own madness."

"Well, tell me then, how did she get the computer out of our offices and then out of the building without being seen by somebody that night?"

"She ordered a master key when she served on the building security committee," she explained. "The police have a record of that, and she used that key to enter the main office to steal the computer. Someone dragged the carton across the floor while she held the door, then the two of them carried the carton down to her office where it remained that night. The university police identified her pickup by chance in the parking lot behind the building the next morning, but she did not have classes that day and the secretaries said she did not come in for her mail. That morning she pulled up to the dock and loaded the computer into the pink pickup."

"More, more, this is circumstantial evidence."

"Correct, but the units of electric power she used at her home have increased since the computer was stolen, more than twelve kilowatt hours a month, which is what a new color tube would use, but she does not own a new set and the increase is closer to a computer than anything else," she explained. Tulip ordered coffee and then continued her oral stories. "Her telephone records show an increase in long distance calls, which could be associated with the use of a computer modem, and she purchased computer supplies for the same model of computer that was stolen, and she made her first charges at that store on the day after the computer was stolen."

"How on earth did you find that out?"

"The oral tradition," she mocked and nibbled her sandwich.

"Now what?" asked Terrocious.

"Tell her what you have learned, and promise her

that no one will know if she returns the computer she borrowed, but remember, she does not seem eager to hear male voices."

"Borrowed is the functional word here," he said, "and if she refuses, then we have no choice but to turn over the information to the university police. What do you think she will do?"

"You're a sexist, of course," she mocked, "and she's gay, and a victim who harvests owl heads, which means she will never appreciate your politics on this one."

"We could borrow back the computer," he said and moved down in the chair. Terrocious shaded his eyes with his hands and watched the muscles on her neck and cheeks move when she sipped her coffee. "That's what we can do, borrow it back one night, that would take care of the problem, no report to the police, no criminal investigation to embarrass the department, and no more problem."

"Would she sue?"

"Embellish the dead head stories and she might."

"Do you like windmills?" asked Tulip.

Eternal Flame Browne

SISTERS in the HARDWOODS

Sister Eternal Flame invited three nuns from the convent to visit the baronage and to attend the Fourth of July celebration on the White Earth Reservation.

The sisters, harnessed in their wimples and black habits, were solicited by children and tribal women to dance in a slow column around the men and powwow singers. The nuns moved their narrow black oxfords in slow motions to the pained voices and thunder of the drum; their heads were down, their hands were folded, their cheeks were blushed.

Then a thunderstorm approached. Lightning flashed in the distance and thunder drummed over the humid peneplain; the powwow dancers moved to cover when the cool winds brushed the trees and clouds darkened the shallow mission pond.

Eternal Flame and the other sisters hurried over to the old mission and watched the storm from the back porch. The trees turned their leaves and shivered; an isolated red pine was uprooted near the main road. Lightning smacked and branded several trees; streamers rose in the weeds and were seared in a wild electrical bond. Thunder rumbled and trembled on the porch; the sisters huddled in silence.

"Listen," said Sister Eternal Flame.

"What do you hear?" asked the other sisters.

"Someone, a voice, over there."

"Must be the wind."

"There, did you hear that?"

"Yes, it is a voice."

"But where?"

"Listen," repeated Eternal Flame.

"Someone is calling for help."

"From the house?"

"Sisters, someone is calling for help from the woods," said Eternal Flame. "Listen, that sounds like a child's voice."

The wild wind lashed the trees and waves of rain washed the porch; hail stones drummed the wood, dashed on rivulets down to a woodland sea.

Eternal Flame removed her shoes, lifted her habit and bounced down the stairs into the water. She turned near the white birch and waved to the sisters who waited in silence on the porch. "Come, the rain is wild, so wild," she shouted and then she raised her head, opened her mouth. The sisters hesitated and then rushed into the rain to search for a child lost in the woods, a wild adventure on the reservation.

The sisters listened to the distant voice and then waded into the dark hardwoods. The high white pine had tamed the wind but currents hummed and whistled down the branches. The nuns wandered under the thunderstorm;

their wet habits were lambent, darker near the tree trunks. Lightning burned behind them and thunder roared overhead.

"The worst has passed," said one nun.

"Where are we?"

"Listen," whispered Eternal Flame, and then she leaned toward the voice. "We're closer. Listen, over there, near the creek."

The sisters found a twelve-year-old boy pinned under a tree on the bank of a rain-swollen creek. The boy shivered when the nuns surrounded him; he cried and pointed to his right thigh which was pinched between two fallen trees.

"How on earth did you get here?" asked Eternal Flame. She held his head and brushed his wet hair back. The other sisters examined his leg; he was bruised, but no bones were broken.

"My uncle's new car," he sobbed.

"You came for the powwow?"

"Yes, my uncle's a real singer."

"Well, you're fine now, the storm is over and the rain has stopped," said Eternal Flame. "Here we are at your side." She waved the sisters aside when they tried to raise the tree, and said, "Wait, we'll get to that in a minute." The sisters were confused and waited for an explanation.

"Thank you sister," he whispered.

"You must have been really worried when four nuns, dressed in black, came out of the thunder and lightning to save you," she said and laughed.

"No, that didn't scare me," he said.

"Barefoot nuns who roam in the woods to save boys who are trapped under trees," she said and wrinkled her nose.

"No, you don't do that," he said.

"What's your name?" asked one of the nuns.

"Marsh."

"Marsh what?"

"Marshall Feralson," he whispered.

"Where is your home?"

"Saint Paul, but don't tell my dad."

"Marsh, how did you get here in the woods?" asked Eternal Flame. She pointed at the box elder on his thigh and said, "How did you get under that tree?"

"It fell on me."

"Hit by lightning?"

"No, not that," he said and turned his head from side to side to see who was there, "I cut the tree a little bit and climbed to the top and swung it down, I did it over there too, and this one cracked, it didn't bend and it fell on me."

"You must have been scared, we hardly heard your voice over the rain and thunder back at the mission," said Eternal Flame.

"Sister, we must remove the tree."

"Wait, not yet," pleaded Eternal Flame.

"Wait for what?"

"Marsh can get himself out," she said. "He knows we're here to help him, but he knows he has to help himself first, on his own as best he can."

"Sister, please," a nun pleaded.

"Marsh," shouted Eternal Flame, "you can get out from under that tree on your own." She brushed his cheeks and moved to the other side of the tree. "Now, what's holding your leg?"

"My knee won't go through," he moaned as he pushed against the fallen tree with one foot and tried to pull his leg free. His face was twisted with fear, but he was not in pain.

"Marsh, you can't let fear hold you back, can you?"

asked Eternal Flame. "You came out here to be a brave young man in the woods, and you wouldn't want four nuns to come to your rescue just because you got your leg caught in a tree."

"No, but . . . "

"So, you can figure this out now," she said. "You think about it, how your leg is caught, how to move. You can do it, and just think how proud you'll feel when you get your leg out all by yourself."

"Yes, but . . . "

"So, we know you're here, and we'll be back at the mission right down the creek, the same way you came into the woods," said Eternal Flame. "There's nothing to fear, if you don't show up in about an hour we'll come back to help you, but don't worry, we won't ever tell your dad what happened."

"Wait . . . "

"Now don't be afraid, think about how to move your leg, don't fight it. How would your uncle get himself out from under that tree?"

"Sister, we can't leave him," a nun whispered.

"Never mind," said Eternal Flame. She pushed the other nuns down the path, back toward the mission. Then she stopped and huddled with the other nuns. "Right here," she whispered, "we'll wait right here and watch him to be sure."

Sister Eternal Flame waited with the sisters behind a boulder and told stories about the tribal trickster who lived in a church organ at a mission boarding school on the reservation. "He watched the levers and learned music from the movements inside the organ," she whispered and raised her hands on the cold wet stone, "and soon he hastened the tunes, he raised the bellows, lifted the pads, and anticipated the notes so well that the devoted nun at the console thought the organ was enlivened with the spirit of the creator. She would touch the first few notes, and the rest of the tune was inspired, a true measure, she thought, of her obedience to music.

"However, when the trickster recast the tunes, the nun was sure to shiver with fear. When she played new tunes, the trickster held the notes, released contrapuntal melodies, and the sister was convinced that a devil possessed the organ. She absolved her vainglorious dedication to music and never again touched an organ."

"Sisters, look! He freed himself."

"Marsh, over here, over here," the nuns chanted.

"You were right," he said out of breath, "my knee was caught, and I slid my leg down the tree and out the end, not much to it."

"So, here you are," shouted Eternal Flame.

"When you left," he said and brushed his trousers, "I sorta thought you tricked me, and I did it different and got out because I knew there was a trick about my knee."

"Marsh has his own stories," said Eternal Flame. She bowed and then pinched his shoulder. "Now, maybe you can lead the lost sisters back to the mission where we lost our shoes."

SCAPEHOUSE and the PRESIDENTS

Eternal Flame Browne renounced the convent and returned with two other sisters to the baronage, where she established a new scapehouse for wounded reservation women.

Flame had a wild spirit, and she was much too passionate and adventurous, too sensitive and inspired, to ever be at peace in a habit and a cloister. The abbess had been censorious over her humor and natural blush, her reveries, dash, and her curious manner with children; the renunciation was mutual.

The Patronia Scapehouse was a haven for lonesome and abused women in search of solace on the reservation. Near the entrance and connected to the scapehouse at the base of the crescent, there were four booths where women listen to men and their wild confessions. There were seven cedar houses and solar greenhouses tiered on the south rise of the crescent.

Men were invited to the confessional booths on the rise but never courted in the scapehouses; children spied on the women in the greenhouses and told imaginative stories to their curious brothers. The women cultivated their own vegetables, raised edible flowers, tended chickens and sheep; what bothered most reservation men was that no men mastered these gender adventures. "Unnatural to be without men," muttered the postman who sorted and delivered the scapehouse mail.

Griever de Hocus and Mouse Proof Martin were the first men to enter the confessional booths that summer. These tricksters were their own consolation; they told stories to the women behind the woven cedar screens in the booths. The women were hurried listeners, too eager to hear remorse and contrition; on the other side of the screen, the tricksters unburdened their best humor and revealed their intemperance and carousals in wild stories about other men, women, and mongrels.

Griever opened the confessional season with stories about a scapehouse where weird and sensitive women ate their pet animals and birds. "This scapehouse was located on Callus Road in Cache Center on the Leech Lake Reservation," he announced in the booth. "Benito Saint Plumero, that rash trickster who carried a violet umbrella and traveled with Private Jones and Pure Gumption, two reservation mongrels, told me that the women shared the men who entered their scapehouse, no one had private rights to a man, sort of an open court where even a bluenose postman might vanish with pleasure."

"Your fantasies are not confessions, and this is a place to hear confessions," said the woman behind the cedar screen on the other side of the booth. "Continue, but remember that we are here to absolve your abuse to women, not to encourage what you must think are innocent stories."

"Saint Plumero had a cock as big as a child's arm, it was so huge that the scapehouse women called it their elected president, their president jackson," he said and smacked the leather patches on his trousers.

"Please, save the presidents."

"In fact, they named all the cocks they ever knew after one president or another," said Griever. "Can you imagine what a president hoover or a teddy roosevelt would look like on the rise in the morning?"

"Saint Plumero told me that the women sang 'Hail to the Chief' when they took an interest in an upstanding chief executive," he shouted and laughed so hard that the back of his head bounced on the rough cedar boards. "So, my mysterious confessor, there's more than one way to elect a president in a two-party system."

"Really, this verbal abuse is the very reason we are here to hear your confessions," she said in a stern voice close to the screen. "Please, it is obvious where your mind is, so get on with your confession or make room for a real man."

"Pure Gumption and the other mongrels were spread on the floor, cats hunched on the tables and chairs, and birds perched on miniature orange trees and succulents, and, outside, doves and chickens roosted under mesh on the posts and rails.

"The weirds and sensitives in that scapehouse ate their pets," he repeated with his voice raised on the last three words."The women ate what they lived with, braised mongrel, stuffed kitten, and consumed one another in the end, the consummate reservation scapehouse."

"You are the weird one," she whispered. She paused and then moved closer to the cedar screen and shouted, "Confess or get out, this is not a bus depot."

"Now there you have a real confession," he said with his nose on the screen. Her wild garlic breath remained on the cedar. "How would you like to meet a president grant, polk, or pierce, or a dark horse nominee named de hocus," he teased and then whistled "Hail to the Chief" as he drummed on the side of the cedar booth.

Mouse Proof Martin commenced with real penitence, the first to be heard in the scapehouse booths. He unbosomed his arousal over shoes, lonesome pumps, and then he revealed that he was never in bed without a warm shoe. "Here, listen, this is a soft blue, she was lost behind the bingo parlor last month," he said and tapped the toe on the cedar screen.

"Do you abuse shoes?" asked Eternal Flame. She disguised her voice because she was so eager to hear confessions on the inauguration of the scapehouse booths.

"Never, never," he said and petted the blue. Mouse Proof was not aware that Eternal Flame was behind the screen. "Lost shoes are never abused at my house, shoes are protected and honored, and most of them, sandals, wedgies, pumps, travel with me and get a chance to show their best at museums and colleges, no lost shoe is lonesome on the road with me."

"Do you put men's shoes on pedestals?"

"No, but I heard about a woman in San Francisco who has the world's largest collection of autographed wing tips," he said and tucked the blue in his pocket.

Mouse Proof leaned back on the rough cedar in the scapehouse booth and remembered that he had no abuses to unburden; he had told his sister more than she ever wanted to hear about his collection of lost and lonesome shoes. Once, when he was in boarding school, he stole the narrow black shoes his teacher wore, the time he discovered his name under the organ, but he told her and she forgave him; later, the teacher was so touched that she contributed those precious black shoes to his collection.

He leaned closer to the cedar screen, reassured that he had no abuses to bear or blame, and told stories about Doc Cloud Burst, the taurine urban warrior and creator of the organization named the San Francisco Sun Dancers.

"Cloud Burst was the keeper of urban tribal traditions and the dispenser of downtown descriptive dream names," he said and drummed the cedar. "Doc drummed with a cultural frown, and that was about it for him, until he met Sarah Blue Welcome, the noted author and looter of the Plains Indian Sun Dance.

"When they came together there were more confessions than even you could shake a stick at, even more than you would want to hear. Well, they needed each other more than grass on a playground, this was a love made over the drum, but the problem was her puppet, and guess what his name was?"

"Wounded Knee? What?"

"Four Skin," he announced and laughed. "Now there was a confession made in heaven, a wooden puppet with a feathered head that got more attention than Doc Cloud Burst. He complained in his usual monotone and no one listened, but then he created a new song about how the jealous puppet drowned when he leaped from the Golden Gate Bridge.

"Four Skin, she avowed, was her minimal tribal man, the man whose head was controlled by a woman's fingers," he said and then paused. "Blue Welcome was wild when she had her finger in that wooden head, she was convinced that tribal men had vanished and that what crawled around now and pretended to be men were nothing more than clowns dressed up to look like the invented tribal people in the photographs of Edward Curtis."

"Blue Welcome is welcome at this scapehouse," said Eternal Flame. She applauded and invited him to continue his stories. "What you say is the truth, a real confession."

"How about Four Skin?" asked Mouse Proof.

"The puppet?"

"Do you welcome puppets at the scapehouse?"

"That depends."

"On what?"

"That depends on his head, so continue."

"Cloud Burst beat on his drum and chanted to his urban disciples, 'Return to the oral traditions and listen to the four directions in the cities, live outdoors, on the streets, in parks, under bridges, but not in hotel lobbies, and search for a personal vision everywhere, even in a dumpster' he repeated and repeated over his drum."

"What happened to Blue Welcome?" asked Flame.

"Well, she followed the urban sun dancers around for a few months, compared notes on the old dances, and then there was trouble," said Mouse Proof. "Token White, the blonde disciple who was an expert with bows and arrows, a real throwback in loose braids, shot Four Skin right between the glass eyes, and his plastic head shattered, teeth here, eyeballs over there, gruesome sight, but no one was really sad about his death, in fact, the urban sun dance disciples cheered the violent death of the puppet.

"Blue Welcome was shattered too," he continued. "She tried to glue him back together, but each time she got his eyes in place and his smile right, someone would crush his head again. Token White threw his eyes into the sea and finally the blind puppet was in too many pieces to be put back together again."

"One of the sisters at the convent had a male puppet," said Eternal Flame. "He started out as a simple priest, but then we made him a real man and passed him around at night."

"Who's there? Who are you?"

"Never mind."

"Sister Flame, is that you?" he asked, close to the cedar screen. He had not recognized her voice until she mentioned the convent.

"Yes," she whispered and covered her mouth. "Mouse Proof, please, promise me you won't tell anyone about the puppet at the convent." She pressed her right ear to the screen and waited for his answer.

"What about the puppet?"

"Not a word," she demanded, "promise me."

"Promise," he agreed. "Flame, you heard all these stories before. Anyway, sister, it sounds like you should be doing the real confessing."

"Father Mouse Proof, I have sinned," she mocked behind the screen. "Please absolve me for abusing that poor little wooden man, no more puppets for me."

"Hail Mary seven times, my child, and then touch the trees your grandmother Novena Mae named the Stations of the Cross," he responded in a solemn voice. "Keep your fingers out of plastic heads."

"And you keep your hands out of my shoes."

"Remember the lonesome border stories?"

"Marion Halcion?"

"Right, she was the cultural anthropologist, whatever that used to be, who retreated to a summer cabin on a border island in Lake of the Woods," said Mouse Proof.

"She wanted to be isolated," said Flame.

"Isolated she was, but urban escapees are never prepared to duck bears and fight mosquitoes. She strained and shivered through a thunderstorm the first night, but she was all head and tied everything together with her voice, like a missionary on an ant hill.

"She talked out loud even when she ate, between bites, and one night she imitated the loons, and that's when she spent her last words and lost touch, which might have been a good thing if an old trickster had not answered her loon call. He waited at a distance and scared the shit out of her because she thought she was alone on the island," said the trickster. "She was terrified, and to overcome her fear she decided to stare at him, to do whatever he did to her, just as she had learned in college, to imitate the men she feared the most."

"Some of us became nuns," said Flame.

"She followed him through the dense woods, over a narrow channel to his cabin on the next island. She waited at the treeline and watched him, but she could not stop talking to herself. She even made notes on her experience and compared the cultures she had studied."

"She needs a scapehouse."

"Well, the mongrels heard her voice and cornered her between two trees," he said and lowered his voice. "Her terror turned to surprise when the gentle old trickster invited her to his cabin.

"Inside, the cabin whirred and burred in a golden

light with miniature windmills. The entire space was a miniature cultural show with pavilions and dioramas. An electric sign blinked The International Tribal Exposition over the show. The trickster told stories over the condominium dioramas where little white men were dressed in blue suits and their children ate fast food in expensive automobiles. There were collections of bones, white skeletons of archaeologists, relics of anthropologists, cultural abusement parks, and pleasure wheels on the margins."

"Poor anthropologists," said Flame.

"Marion was so excited that she rushed back and told her friends at the university about what she had found and invited them to come with her to see the miniature exposition on the island, her first significant cultural discovery.

"Well, when she got back there with three boatloads of anthropologists, the cabin was empty, the old man was not there," said Mouse Proof. "An immigration officer on the lake explained that a tribal shaman had once lived in the cabin, 'But that was over thirty years ago.'

"The cabin straddled the international border, and while the anthropologists were huddled on the dock, the old trickster appeared in the distance, behind the trees. He smiled, and she smiled back, but she never told the others that he was there."

"Listen, did you ever hear the stories about the mixedblood radicals who were on trial in federal court?" asked Flame.

"More cloud bursts?"

"The San Francisco sun dancers are nothing compared to these clowns," she said and leaned back on the cedar. "They told the jury that 'Living things come from our sacred mother earth, all living things, the green things, the winged things of the air, the four leggeds,' if you can believe that tribal rubbish, and some of the jurors swallowed it whole because they were dressed in leathers and feathers and beads.

"One of the mixedbloods on trial said 'But the important thing in our philosophy is that we believe we're the weakest things on earth, that the two-legged is the weakest thing on earth because we have no direction.' He was right about the 'no direction,' but he would never be drawn to radical politics to become the 'weakest thing on earth.'

"The real killer was when he told the federal jurors that he wanted to share the pain of 'all the female objects of this planet.' Later he added, 'The men warriors would like to share some of the pain that our mothers had when we were born.' So, he became a sun dancer to share the pain of women? Well, then, he can confess to us at the scapehouse."

"Did he really say that in court?"

"Who could invent that radical gibberish?"

"The scapehouse confessors," said Mouse Proof.

"Never, not a word to the unwise."

"Did you ever hear the story about the urban sun dancer and the old trickster, a mixedblood writer at the bar?" he asked.

"What bar?" asked Flame.

"Hello Dolly's in Minneapolis."

"Never been there."

"The old trickster writer listened to an urban sun dancer boast over the sun dance scars on his chest, and he walked to the bar, unbuttoned his flannel shirt, pointed to several scars on his stout chest, and said, 'See those?' The urban sun dancer was impressed and nodded in deference to the elder. 'Chicken pox, nineteen thirty-two' said the old mixedblood and returned to his booth at the back. The skins at the bar hooted and doubled over with laughter."

"What happened to the dancer?"

"Who knows, he probably ran on his sun dance scars and was elected to a tribal government somewhere," said Mouse Proof. "Nowhere I'd want to be, even with good stories and chicken pox."

"Mouse Proof, before we go on, is there anyone else out there waiting to confess something?" asked Eternal Flame.

"Chicken Lips, no one else."

"He licks feet and you collect shoes," she said and laughed, "now there must be a connection and a shared confession there somewhere."

"Mongrels stick together?"

"China and Chicken Lips," she mused. Eternal Flame thought about her sister and the mongrels on the baronage. "Did Griever de Hocus enter a booth?"

"Not for long."

"Listen, would you invite him to come over and tell me his stories about the presidents?" asked Eternal Flame. She brushed her rough hands and examined her fingernails.

"Puppets and presidents?"

"You promised."

"President polk, pierce, or grant?"

"No, perhaps fillmore this time," said Eternal Flame.

Father Mother
Browne

PURE GUMPTION and
the FLAT EARTH SOCIETY

Father Father Mother is a trickster healer. Beneath his warm hands the bored and lonesome are mended and the sick are cured, but the church patriarchs were suspicious and banished the mixedblood priest to a remote parish at Fortuna, North Dakota, where, on a winter night, he was invested a potent member of the Flat Earth Society.

Double Father, as he was known on the baronage when he was ordained, was seldom surprised when cold reason blundered on ecclesiastical rails because he was closer to the animals in a human than he was to the mind of a primate. The trickster was liberated on the prairie and pleased to be a member of the Flat Earth Society with men and women who believed in the plain and evident.

The narrow chapel was perched at the high end of a gravel road two blocks north of a withered bank and one block east of a gun and antique dealer. The bank had failed fifty-four years ago in the same year that Gun and Content

Hanson were married by the last pastor to serve their unincorporated town; that winter the old priest died in a wicked blizzard and the chapel became the main base of the liberal council of the Flat Earth Society.

Gun was proclaimed president and Content was elected treasurer of the international organization that was dedicated to the promotion of the obvious; the empirical landlubbers truth that the earth is flat but not smooth. "No matter what, we got some wrinkles way out on the edges," the liberal elders allowed, "but this earth sure is flat right down to that heartless sea." The trickster priest was the only member who had traveled more than twenty miles from the center of town; ten more miles out and the earth might have been thrown into orbit on the prairie.

"Damn, the church is back," shouted Gun.

"Back where?" asked Content.

"Here, we got our priest back."

"My God, never thought this day would come, fifty-four years since the last priest, and our marriage, and the last big storm," she whispered and turned the lock on the back door. She had not locked the door since the time three men had escaped from the state prison.

Gun and Content tiptoed on the gravel road behind the priest who carried a black portmanteau and a pennant case. White Lies and Pure Gumption, two mongrels from the baronage, barked in the weeds near the outhouse behind the chapel. The mosquitoes were heinous at dusk. "Father, welcome back," said Gun. "Wait, that door hasn't been opened since the last priest was here," he warned as the priest turned the wide brass key in the lock. "When we took over, we used the back door all these years."

Angels carved on the oak panels cocked their weathered eyes and braced the double doors. Gun butted the center, then the priest pressed his shoulder on a rimrose breast and the two men beamed, but the doors would not open. The mongrels pawed and barked. Content waved the men and mongrels aside; she pushed one side and pulled the other. The double doors screeched open and separated the spider webs that had sealed the cracked panels.

The chapel smelled of stale cigar smoke. The rose windows at each end were clouded over with webs and dead insects. A huge black patriarchal cross was decorated with several broadsides that announced the annual celebrations of the International Flat Earth Society in Fortuna. "Come to North Dakota, the Best Corner on the Edge." He cleaned the windows and polished the cross.

Double Father transformed the chapel with herbs and wild flowers, common birds, and miniature windmills that his sister had built for the occasion. The chapel was a wild haven: birds nested in the wooden nave; mongrels healed on the communion table; and three windmills whirred and burred over the verdant chancel. The steeple was painted in rainbow colors and the chapel was christened the Cathedral of the Flat Earth.

Pure Gumption, the shaman mongrel who glowed and healed with her paws and tongue, inspired the priest more than dead letter supplication and absolution. This mongrel, who was abandoned on the baronage and ran with White Lies, taught the trickster the animal art of healing with the paws.

That summer the lonesome and sick came over the prairie to be healed by the shaman mongrels and a mixed-blood priest. There were hundreds of families camped near the river and on the distant meadows. The trickster demonstrated how to scream into panic holes; at night their voices carried to the chapel and the bedrooms in the town. Content cursed the wanderers and closed the windows. "Sick people," she whispered to her husband, "sick and lonesome howlers like the rest of us in this dead town."

Double Father and the mongrels praised the lonesome on the run and healed the sick in the chapel when the sun dropped over the edge of the earth. The natural time to heal was at dusk when the trees, birds, and animals spread their enormous shadows.

Pure Gumption glowed on the communion table; she laid her paws on the lonesome and licked the sick. On the other side of the chancel the priest liberated and healed the animals and birds that were penned inside the humans. White Lies moved down the narrow pews and pushed her wet nose under dresses, into moist groins. The elders scratched her head and she smiled and licked their arthritic thighs; the touch of a mongrel lowered their blood pressure, which had been elevated by guilt and television evangelists.

One humid evening the low sun bowed through a rose window and severed the communion table. The birds twittered in the nave and swooped down on the mongrels; the air cavities in their bones were sensitive to the approach of a storm. Thunderclouds billowed in the distance and towed ominous shrouds over the prairie.

The wind roared and the nave beams strained. Wild lightning sheared weeds on the meadow, and thunder boomed in the chapel. The priest herded the sick and lonesome to a dark storm shelter; there, the mongrels barked at the thunder and the humans told stories until the storm had passed.

The Cathedral of the Flat Earth lost a few wooden staves from the steeple and the outhouse was overturned, but there was no real harm; however, trees were down and most houses in the town were damaged by the storm. Windows were shattered, trailers were overturned, and the water tower listed to the east.

Gun and Content summoned members of the Flat Earth Society to witness their house; the wind had moved the small house several inches on the foundation. The water and sewer pipes were twisted and exposed; there were minor leaks, but no breaks.

"Help me move it back on the foundation," shouted Gun. He shivered over the words, and his bleached cheeks trembled with fear. "Help me, do something."

"Bulldozers."

"No, house jacks might do it."

"We can push," said Double Father.

"You caused us enough trouble," he moaned. Gun glanced at the older members and nodded his head. "This is my house, not the chapel, so leave it to me."

"We never had a storm this bad before, not since the last priest was here," said the manager of a gasoline station. He bowed his head and held one ear.

"Never, never this bad," shouted Content. She was perched on her elbows at the bathroom window. "Father, you and those wild mongrels brought us some real bad luck this time."

"You said it," chimed the others.

"First, those strangers come here for some cure, and now this storm," said Gun. "Father, you best stand aside now, this is a man's job."

"But this is the Flat Earth Society," pleaded the priest.

"Not anymore," said Gun.

"We just had a vote and changed the rules," said Content. Her voice vibrated on the plastic window screen and released rainwater from the squares.

Double Father was wounded by the sudden rescission of his membership in the Flat Earth Society. He moved back with the mongrels and listened to the men estimate the methods to restore the house. While the men measured the distance to the nearest stout tree, an anchor for a house jack, the priest touched the mongrels. His hands were warmed, his breath was heated, slow and determined.

Pure Gumption glowed in the wet weeds behind the house. White Lies bounced in circles and barked into shallow panic holes. The Flat Earth Society members shooed the mongrels and continued their measurements.

The mixedblood placed his hands on the corner of the house, pressed his shoulder to the wet clapboard, and pushed with the power of an old tribal shaman. His hands glowed on the rough boards and the house shuddered. Pure Gumption butted the back of his legs and pawed his heels. White Lies barked at the white light that surrounded the trickster and the corner of the house.

"What the hell is he doing?" asked Gun.

"He's pissing on the corner."

"No, he's possessed."

"What the hell is this? Call the state patrol!"

"My God!" screamed Content.

"Jesus Christ."

"Wait, wait," shouted Gun. "Listen to that, the house is moving, that crazy priest is moving our whole damned house back on the foundation."

The windows trembled, the walls shivered, and the floor joists roared as the mixedblood pushed the house back several inches on the foundation. Mosquitoes swarmed the silent men behind the house. Content locked the windows and doors.

Later, the members of the Flat Earth Society gathered at the chapel to apologize to the priest. The double doors were locked so the members entered at the back. The inside smelled of cigar smoke as it had before the priest arrived. The birds and their nests in the nave were down.

The plants had vanished and the rose windows were clouded once again with spider webs. The black patriarchal cross folded a double shadow over the communion table. The trickster priest had tacked a hand-printed message on the cross; he invited the members to "heal the lost and lonesome, mend the houses last, and no priest will ever bother you again."

The LAST LECTURE on the EDGE

Father Mother Browne renounced the priesthood and returned to the baronage, where he became a public mourner and celebrant at funerals on the reservation; he was inspired by the spontaneous paternosters and entreaties at tribal wakes and over the graves. The survivors besought the dead to remember a better past, humor over disease, mythic stories over incurious studies, a woodland renaissance.

Father Mother mourned through the winter, and then on the summer solstice he was moved in a dream to ordain a tavern and sermon center; the Last Lecture was built on a watershed below the scapehouse at the south end of the baronage. The urban mixedbloods who had moved to the reservation were summoned to carve a stone precipice behind the tavern, named the Edge of the White Earth. There, seven modern telephone booths were mounted in a row with double doors, one opened over the precipice.

Those who subscribed to step over the edge were allowed one last call before they dropped into their new names and social identities.

"There ain't no such thing as a last lecture," said the postman, who was troubled over the increased mail service to the baronage. "My wife says something like that, she says, 'These are my last words,' but she never means it."

"The last lecture, one at a time," said Father Mother.

"If you don't mind me saying so," said the postman as he cocked his hat, "you people are a strange lot with those booths, the scapehouse, and now this place."

"Shakespeare said that once."

"Did he now."

"In his last lecture," said Father Mother, "he listed one by one all the strange things he saw around him, once he saw it and named it in a play, that was the end of it, nothing more to say."

"Well, he was on to something there, but he never delivered the mail to this place," said the postman. "If you start something else out here, make it the last letter."

The Last Lecture was a circular cedar structure with a bar and booths on one side and a theater, with tables and chairs, on the other; visitors were invited to present their sermons and last lectures on the theater stage. Mixedblood educators, tribal radicals, writers, painters, a geneticist, a psychotaxidermist, and various pretenders to the tribe took the microphone that summer and told the bold truth; these lost and lonesome mixedbloods practiced their new names, made one last telephone call to their past, and then dropped over the edge into a new wild world.

Marie Gee Hailme was dressed in paisley velvet and black lace when she raised the microphone to deliver her last lecture; her narrow mouth moved in a monotone. More than a hundred tribal people from communities on the reservation crowded into the sermon center to hear the director of urban tribal education, the first to unburden her vanities that season; even the postman was at the bar that night. She mumbled that the tribal values she had introduced in classrooms were amiss and biased.

"My skin is dark," she whispered, "you can see that much, but who, in their right mind, would trust the education of their children to pigmentation?" Marie Gee held the microphone too close to her mouth; her voice hissed in the circular tavern. "Who knows how to grow up like an Indian? Tell me that, and who knows how to teach values that are real Indian?

"I was orphaned and grew up in a church boarding school, so they trusted me, because of their guilt over my dark skin, and put me in charge of developing classroom materials about Indians," she said and lowered the microphone.

"I went all over the state lecturing about Indian values to help white teachers understand how Indian students think and why they drop out of school, but once, right in the middle of a lecture, an Indian student asked me, 'What kind of Indians are you talking about? There aren't no Indians like that out here on our reservation.' I realized that I was describing an invented tribe, my own tribe that acted out my hang-ups, which had nothing to do with being a person stuck in a public school.

"I was telling white teachers that Indians never look you in the eye and Indians never touch. Can you believe that I was teaching that as the basic values and behavior of Indians? Those weren't values, they were my hang-ups, and they had nothing to do with anybody else. My pigmentation and degrees made me an expert on Indians. Would you believe that my dissertation was on Indian values? My hang-ups became the values, and then I compared them to other cultures. White academics loved it, the whole thing made sense to teachers, but it had nothing to do with Indians, because the Indian students never understood what I was saying about the values imposed on them.

"So, I pulled back, turned around last month, and looked at myself and the other Indian teachers, at what we had been doing, and I discovered the obvious, yes, the obvious," she said in the same tone and loosened her padded velvet coat. "We were all mixedbloods, some light and some dark, and married to whites, and most of us had never really lived in reservation communities. Yes, we suffered some in college, but not in the same way as the Indian kids we were trying to reach, the ones we were trying to keep in school when school was the real problem. But there we were, the first generation of Indian education experts, forcing our invented curriculum units, our idea of Indians, on the next generation, forcing Indian kids to accept our biased views.

"That curriculum crap we put together about Indians was just as boring and inaccurate as the white materials we were revising and replacing. We pretended to do this for Indian kids, in their interests, but were we really honest?"

"Never, no, never," a man shouted at the bar.

"I think not. We did it for the money and the power bestowed on us by liberal whites. We should have trashed the schools, not ourselves with the delusions that we were helping Indian students. We were helping ourselves and the schools hold on to their power over children, and all the while we pretended to teach Indian pride. Can you believe that?"

"Pride quit school with me," the man shouted.

"Compromise, the kind that leads to self hatred, is what we were really teaching. I should have listened, the

Indian kids knew better, but we used them to do good and get ahead.

"So, here I am giving my last lecture, and tomorrow I'll walk over the Edge of the Earth with a new name and a bus ticket to a crowded place out by the ocean for a new start at my life," she said and tapped her finger on the microphone. "Thanks to Father Mother, I'm through with my ideas about Indian values and education. Too much of that crap could kill an ordinary spirit."

Marie Gee saluted the crowd with the microphone; she bowed to the former priest and then ordered a round of drinks for everyone in the Last Lecture. She was applauded and cheered at the bar; two stout men in a booth raised their straw hats in the seven directions and ordered seven more bottles of beer.

Coke de Fountain waited at the bar in silence; his massive shoulders shuddered when he listened to the educator end her career. He ordered a double gin and then entered his name as a last lecturer. The crowd roared with derision when his name was printed on the board over the noted author Homer Yellow Snow and several other last lecturers scheduled that night.

De Fountain was an urban pantribal radical and dealer in cocaine. His tribal career unfolded in prison, where he studied tribal philosophies and blossomed when he was paroled in braids and a bone choker. He bore a dark cultural frown, posed as a new colonial victim, and learned his racial diatribes in church basements; radical and stoical postures were tied to federal programs. The race to represent the poor started with loose money and ran down to the end with loose power. When the dash was blocked, the radical restored his power over the poor with narcotics; he inspired his urban warriors with cocaine.

Father Mother waved his hands and called attention

to the importance of last lectures. "Our next lecturer, the second in line, needs no introduction. You have heard his mixedblood wrath in the cities, you have seen his wild face on television, and some have whispered his name in anger. Now, on our stage, the man who took the most and gave the least back, the mad deacon of the urban word warriors, has agreed to deliver his last lecture on the run."

Coke cleared his throat, a wild rumble, and squeezed loud clicks from the microphone with his scarred hands. The audience hissed and sneered and then waited in silence; bottles, mouths, and hands were cocked.

"Wounded Knee was the beginning in our calendar, the first year of the new warriors," he roared and pounded the microphone in his hand. "We went back and took that place, it was ours, the chapel and the graves, we earned it back, and we did it for the elders, so the elders could be proud again."

"Bullshit," a woman shouted from a booth.

"We always listen to our elders," Coke shouted back and waved one hand in a circle. "We did what the elders wanted us to do, we protected their sacred traditions."

"You did it for the money and blondes," said an elder at the bar. He laughed at the radical and mocked his hand movements. "Money and women, that's why you went to Wounded Knee and that's what will put you back in prison, because you never did anything for anybody."

"Our young people are destroyed in racist schools," he roared, and he sputtered and moved closer with the microphone pressed on his mouth like a rock singer. "Who are you to tell me anything? What have you ever done to save our children?"

"Wounded Knee we will remember," said the elder, "but you, and your mouth, we want to forget, we want to forget what you have done to our memories."

"De Fountain, he's the one who saved our children with drugs, and taught them how to hate," said a tribal woman at a table close to the stage. She turned and shouted to the others, "This man never saved anyone, not even himself. He's evil, he hates himself, he's got no vision, he's a killer of our dreams."

"My conscience is clean. . . . "

"Your conscience is cocaine," the woman screamed.

"I came here to talk about racism and genocide. Genocide!" he barked into the microphone. "What have you ever done but sit on a bar stool and bring disgrace to our sacred mother earth."

"Your mother earth is a blonde," the tribal woman said, and then she moved closer to the radical. "You use women and pretend to love mother earth, but you would rather have a blond woman than live on a reservation. You let a white foster family care for your children while you parade around and hate whites. Why don't you take care of your own kids before you worry so much about mother earth?" The woman stood below him on the aisle with her hands on her hips and chanted, "woman hater, woman hater."

"I don't have to listen to this," he moaned and moved back from the tables, a man in retreat. His power had eroded and now he was alone, cornered in his own lecture by those who had waited in silence on the reservation. "Wounded Knee told the world that we were proud people once again, and we did that for you, we saved our children from the disgrace of white racism."

"Wounded Knee saved you, no one but you and your pack of worthless downtown warriors," said the elder at the bar. "You can't even save your own red ass without a white lawyer, federal money, and now that damn microphone."

"Listen here," he bellowed and aimed the microphone at the old man, "I don't have to give my last lecture here, so pack up your backward ideas and forget it. Down your beer old man and forget it. You've got no pride, there's nothing left in you."

Coke de Fountain dropped the microphone on the floor and the sound rumbled in the tavern. "This is not my last lecture. Never, never," he told Father Mother. "Why should I give my last lecture to those tomahawks?" Coke threw the envelope with his new name at the crowd; he sneered over his shoulder on the way out, slammed the door, and hurried over to the booths at the scapehouse.

Homer Yellow Snow, the spurious tribal author, arrived in a brown limousine minutes behind the radical who withdrew his last lecture. The author told his chauffeur, a muscular blonde, to wait for him on the road below the telephone booths at the Edge of the White Earth.

"Father Mother?" asked Yellow Snow.

"Not me," said the elder at the bar. "He's over there at a table, the one in the white suit and black collar. Would you believe that man was a priest once?"

"Would you believe I was once an Indian?" he asked the elder and then ordered a bottle of white wine to celebrate his wild conversion.

"No, but who asked?"

"No one worth mentioning," the author allowed.

"Yellow Snow, you're here," said Father Mother. He rushed over to the author at the bar. "Please, join us at a table before you begin your lecture."

"Do you have the documents?"

"The whole bundle," responded Father Mother. "Change of names, driver's license, credit cards, voter registration, the new you over the last past."

Patronia retains certain civil records, as several treaties provide, such as birth, death, marriage, and divorce. The Last Lecture expanded these common civil records to include surnames, licenses, legal residences, and other documents demanded by those who deliver their last lectures on the baronage.

Homer Yellow Snow demanded three new names, a recorded tribal death in an auto accident, a wake and burial of his past on the reservation; these were provided at a much higher cost than the usual admissions to the new world.

"So, what's your new name?" asked Marie Gee.

"Not a chance," the author said with a nervous smile. "No one but my chauffeur will ever connect my new names to the past."

"What a pity, we might have pretended," she sighed.

"That's the theme of my lecture."

"Did you prepare your last lecture?" asked Father Mother.

"Yes, but on the way over I read it to my chauffeur and changed my mind," said Yellow Snow. "This time my last lecture will be spontaneous and the prepared speech will become my press release, along with the notice that I was killed tonight in a tragic automobile accident."

"Death kits for the authors," said Marie Gee.

"Pretend Indians," he whispered.

"The late Yellow Snow," announced Father Mother. "We are honored to have one of the best-known tribal authors here to deliver his last lecture."

"Ladies and gentlemen," said the author with the microphone in both hands. He wore turquoise bracelets, a thick silver beltbuckle, and a double beaded necklace. "You are about to hear the last, or rather the first, honest words of Homer Yellow Snow, author, artist, historian, tribal philosopher, and last but not least, a pretend Indian.

"Within the hour, my friends, I will be dead on a reservation road, and the Indian author you thought you knew will step over the edge and become a Greek, an Italian, perhaps a Turk, but no more will I be your Indian."

"Spare me the heartbreak," said a tribal man in a booth with two blondes. "You never were anything to me, white or whatever you pretended to be."

"Let the man talk," said Marie Gee.

"This last lecture actually began several years ago when a mixedblood writer questioned my tribal identity, he challenged an autobiographical essay I had submitted for publication in an anthology," said the author in a sonorous voice. His words were practiced, measured on a line. "You see, my tribal identities were pretentious, my blood recollections were artificial, at best, and this mixedblood writer detected how impossible were my autobiographical experiences. He told the editor of the book to either correct or drop my essay.

"He saw right through my invented tribal childhood, he detected the flaws in my asserted poverty, in my avowed tribal identities, and he was secure enough in his own experiences to challenge me. I should thank him for driving me to this, my last lecture.

"That was the turning point, the beginning of my revisions, double revisions since then, preparations for my last lecture, and now over the edge with my new names. I have Father Mother, this extraordinary man, to thank for an opportunity to start a new life with a proper public confession.

"Save one or two academic skeptics, I had the entire white and tribal worlds believing in me as a writer and historian, and eating out of my hand as a philosopher, especially when I raised foundation support for films and tribal seminars," he said and then paused to consider the audience. The ticktock of the tavern clock measured the silence. Two men in a booth peeled the labels from several beer bottles and rolled the moist paper into wads.

"What other culture could be so easily duped?" asked Homer Yellow Snow. "Listen, all it took was a little dark skin, a descriptive name, turquoise and silver, and that was about it, my friends. With that much, anyone could become an Indian."

"Whites are the real victims," the elder shouted.

"What about white people?" asked Yellow Snow.

"Dupe the whites," the elder answered from the end of the bar. "We duped the whites more than they duped us, we even duped them to think they were duping us."

"Really," mocked the author.

"You duped yourself to pretend you were like us," said a woman in a booth. "You're the white, you're the victim, and that's your problem not ours, so who's the dupe?"

"So there, my tribal friends," he said with hesitation, "you have my story, the adventures of a pretend Indian who published his way to the top with turquoise and a tribal mask, and all of you needed me, white and tribal, to absolve your insecurities and to convince the world that you were more than a lost whisper in a museum, more than a stick figure on birchbark or a faded mark on buffalo hide."

"Yellow Snow, hit the edge," said a disabled man at the bar. He wobbled between the tables with bottles in his hands. "This here is a real skin on your trail, and we got a claim to piss on some of that phoney blood, mister white eyes."

"If you knew who you were, why did you find it so easy to believe in me?" the author asked and then answered, "because you too want to be white, and no matter what you say in public, you trust whites more than you trust Indians, which is to say, you trust pretend Indians more than real ones."

Father Mother handed Homer Yellow Snow his bundle of new names and identities, an invoice for conversion services, and escorted the author through the back door to the booths and the precipice. Yellow Snow telephoned his chauffeur, removed his turquoise, bone choker, beads, and stepped over the edge into the new world with three new names.

The Last Lecture served thirteen tribal pretenders and several hundred mixedbloods in the first few months the tavern was opened. Father Mother provided new names and identities through the baronage for a nominal fee. The cost was so low, and the last lecture such a solace, that some mixedbloods returned several times to unburden their new identities for an even newer name; the last lectures, for some, became an annual ritual. Some mixedbloods, however, belied their own last lectures, balked at the booth and the edge, and returned to their past with dubious resolve and courage.

Coke De Fountain turned his resistence to a new name into a competitive business. The racial freebooter opened the Very Last Plea, a fry bread parlor and tribal desert house, where he provided new descriptive names, cocaine, and membership in the New Breed, a radical urban movement.

Father Mother introduced each last lecturer and listened to their conversions; he endured the returns and repetitions, but one night he interrupted a genetic acarid engineer and delivered his own last lecture.

See See Arachnidan, a mixedblood recluse who had moved back to the reservation, revealed the parasitic testicle ticks that she had bred to attack authoritarian personalities: police officers, court officials, some teachers, and federal agents. "One testick bite causes a rare disease. In an instant, men stutter like rich liberals on the Fourth of July. My testicks are aroused by certain male hormones in groin sweat," she said as the microphone died. She was told to sit down and be silent.

Father Mother stared at the audience for several minutes, and then he delivered his own last lecture. "Listen, I have listened long enough to last lectures of the lost and lonesome. Now it is my time to choose a new name and walk over the edge," he said and placed the microphone on a chair. The audience cheered when he removed his black collar, white coat and trousers. He turned in circles and then walked backward in his shorts and white shoes out the back door of the tavern.

Father Mother was the last lecturer at the Last Lecture; he wrapped himself in a plain brown blanket, entered the telephone booth, and called his mother at the scapehouse. The former priest laughed in the booth and decided to become a woman with a new name in a new wild world.

Slyboots Browne

TRIBE GAMES
and GHOST COURTS

Slyboots Browne was the most clever and devious trickster on the White Earth Reservation. His imagination hovered with no halters, no margins in his worldviews; he was unbound, a wild dreamer with no practical burdens, an avian heir to the tribal baronage.

The trickster was sixteen when he read the *History of the Ojibway Nation* by William Warren. The mixed-blood historian and legislator revealed a sacred copper plate with eight marks, one for each generation of tribal families on Madeline Island in Lake Superior. "By the rude figure of a man with a hat on his head, placed opposite one of these indentations, was denoted the period when the white race first made his appearance among them. This mark occurred in the third generation, leaving five generations which had passed away since that important era in their history."

Slyboots imagined that first tribal encounter with whites and fashioned several copper plates, which he sold as historical relics to summer tourists on the reservation. Later, he hammered and carved a saucer on which he incised the signatures of monarchs and presidents. The signatories declared that the woodland tribes have an absolute right to gamble on their land. With the copper saucer in hand, he started the first bingo games in an orange circus tent on the baronage. The copper saucer was his prime masterstroke; the bingo operation was his second; his third trickster scheme was a coup de main.

Bingo enlivened tired reservation communities and stimulated lonesome tribal elders; at the same time, the games drew the rude attention of the government. Federal agents were not impressed with the copper saucer as paramount documentation. Meanwhile, the games spurred the interest and greed of organized white gamblers who thought they could manipulate a mixedblood to their advantage.

Slyboots, however, outwitted the government, elected tribal politicians, and organized crime, in two clever moves. First, he sold the rights to bingo on the reservation and, second, he founded a new game of chance based on lotto; one month later bingo was suspended on the reservation.

"Thirteen under the bee."

"R seven."

"Tee four, that's four under the tee."

"Tribe," a tribal woman shouted.

"We have a tribe," the tribe caller announced. "Hold your cards until we verify the numbers. Yes, yes, we do have a tribe, the lady is a winner."

"Tribe is the same game as bingo," the trickster explained later, "but when bingo drew too much attention, I sold out and changed the name to tribe, which is still a game of chance in some reservation communities."

"You were only sixteen, what did you do with all the money?" asked a blond banker who was doing research on mixedblood entrepreneurs and reservation economics for the Federal Reserve Bank.

"First, I hired the best lawyer in the cities to represent me, no matter what I did, for ten years," said Slyboots. "I paid him a thousand in advance, which was nothing to him, but I knew he would be impressed with my unusual adolescent enthusiasm, if nothing else, I was worth a few good stories over lunch or at his cocktail parties."

"What stories did he tell?" asked the banker.

"Well, let me tell you about the time we established the bone courts, or bone head law, to protect tribal graves," said the trickster as he examined his hands.

"Are you serious?"

"Archaeologists robbed the graves of our ancestors, stole their bones," he said on cue. "We pleaded with them to show common respect for the dead, but these dead head scientists defended their rights. Their rights!"

"What rights?" asked the banker.

"Their scientific rights to the dead, the tribal dead. None of them would dare steal bones from white graves, so we pleaded with the court to represent bones, the rights of skeletons to remain buried."

"What happened?"

"The judge threw the case out because he ruled that a skeleton did not have legal standing in a federal court," said Slyboots. "So, we appealed and argued that corporations have rights and who are corporations? Riparian rights are based on water, and trees, children, air, and snail darters have legal standing, we argued, and convinced the judge that tribal skeletons had a right to be represented in court.

Now the archaeologists must answer to tribal skeletons and their lawyers in bone court or at a federal ghost hearing."

"Ghost hearing?"

"Well, some tribal lawyers pretended to hear voices and argued that their cases were prepared by the skeletons they represented, ghost writers in a bone court. You should read what the archaeologists said to defend their rights to dig up tribal skeletons.

"We demanded at a ghost hearing that the bones stolen from tribal burial grounds and stashed in the Museum of Natural History at the Smithsonian Institution and in the Field Museum of Natural History at Chicago be reburied."

"But don't they have a right to prehistory?"

"Whose prehistories, oral or written?" the trickster shouted. "Listen, some of those skeletons were stolen from Old Walpi at First Mesa by the Stanley McCormick Expedition, tribal spirits sacked from the Hopi. No one has a right to claim the past with a racist calendar.

"One archaelogist said, 'Your Honor, the value of scientific information, such as Indian dietary habits, migratory routes, and diseases, is much more important than a burial, and worse yet would be reburial.'

"We responded that archaeological research on tribal bones is racist and a morbid preoccupation with colonialism, a colonial necrophilia," said the trickster with a smile. "First the land, then our religions, material cultures, and now the last colonial merit badge is to claim a right to our bones.

"Then a cultural anthropologist testified, 'What's all the fuss about? We're no better than animals and birds, we all return to the earth. Why so much trouble over our bones?'

"Throw yours to the bears, then, we told him, but

remember, animals and birds don't bury their dead to avoid the vultures, but we have to worry about archaeologists pounding around in the dust in the name of science."

"You certainly are convincing," said the blond banker, "but could we talk now about money rather than bones, your bingo and tribe business on reservations?"

"Of course, what else," he sighed. "I incorporated and copyrighted the new tribe game, which I knew would lead to legal battles with the bingo people, and directed that all the profits from tribe be invested in tribal scholarships and false teeth."

"False teeth?"

"Mormons did that once, the missionaries always have a whole smile. I got the idea from them and provided free partials and false teeth to the elders," the trickster said and turned a wild smile on the banker. "My mother got a set from them and that whole smile changed her life, believe me."

"What else did you do with your money?"

"I invested enough money in stocks to cover my education," he said and counted thousands outloud. "Private school and then on to college."

"You're not exactly the poor Indian from the reservation we read so much about," said the blond banker as she closed a small notebook.

"Well now, you're not exactly the evil white banker from the cities we read about either," said the trickster. "Did it ever occur to you that everything whites have been told by tribal people was imagined, were trickster stories?"

"Mixedblood stories," she smirked.

"Red hash, miscrible tribes, mule imbued, are the words, and all the more reason to be wary," the trickster whispered and raised his dark eyebrows. "Listen, why don't you visit our confessional booths at the scapehouse before you leave, my sister is there ready to hear your racial theories."

"Touchy, touchy," she said. "Would you talk more about economics on the reservation? What else did you do with the money you earned from games?"

"You'll like this," he said. "I established a bird hospital in the cities and trained tribal people to care for wounded birds."

"Now you are a trickster," she said.

"Believe me, a real bird hospital."

"What on earth for?"

"Now you're with me," he sighed. "Because urban whites have so much to learn from tribal people, so much to learn about birds and those lonesome shadows in the urban trees."

"So, what does that mean?"

"We are avian dreamers," he whispered and leaned to one side and then the other. "When we heal a bird we mend the wind, our lost shadows, a wounded bird is a lonesome heart."

Slyboots told true stories to the blond banker that summer; however, that part about stock investments was embellished. He won scholarships to attend a private school and college and earned his board with the tribe game.

The summer before he entered college, he christened three tribe boats on the international border and invited tourists to a scenic game of chance. The season was an enormous success; again, when governments were about to intervene to control a tribal business, he sold the boats and business to a prosperous international travel corporation for cash and a percentage of the games. Tribe is still a vacation game of chance on the border islands.

MICROLIGHTS and
AVIAN DREAMS

Slyboots Browne graduated from Dartmouth College with a degree in economics and Native American studies. His wise and clever manner was a lodestone in a racist institution; he was not too dark to bear the nod in private clubs, but he was dark enough to remember his trickster cues in public.

His honors thesis, "Dirt Cheap Toilet Seats and Camouflage: A Study of Military Contracts on American Indian Reservations,"won the senior student patriot award and was published in the prestigious alumni magazine. This honor brought his name to the attention of influential graduates.

The student president of the patriot committee at the college was the favorite grandson of the secretary of defence; more important, he was a student pilot and taught the trickster how to fly a biplane in less than a hour.

Slyboots sold a college tribe franchise the month before he graduated, invested the money in a biplane, and flew back to the baronage that summer. He circled the crescent four times, buzzed the cedar cabins, and landed on the dirt road near the scapehouse, too close to the postman.

"This is a mail route, not a damn airport," the postman shouted over the roar of the engine. "Stop that thing, stop it right now, I tell you!"

The trickster parked the biplane behind the Last Lecture, cut the engine, and leaped to the ground with a flourish; he was a college graduate, an educated mixedblood, dressed in a leather suit. "You're just the man I want to see."

"Slyboots, so it's you."

"How would you like to be the first reservation postman in the airmail business?" the trickster asked and flashed a comic smile.

"Never mind," he said with determination. "But that's how you people will get your mail in the future if you land that thing around me again. I swear, I'll send your mail on a windstorm, you can bet on it, mister."

"Listen, I'm back for good now," said the trickster as he removed his gloves and handed the postman two business cards. "Here are my two new addresses at the baronage."

"Patronia International Airport, what on earth is that?" the postman asked. He turned the card over and rubbed his thumb on the raised letters.

"Not what, but *where*?"

"Where then?"

"Right on that narrow meadow back behind the crescent, as soon as I level the land for a runway and build a new hanger," said the trickster with his hands deep in his pockets.

"You people are insane, without a doubt, insane," mumbled the postman, as he sorted several letters. "No wonder our government never honored the treaties. Who would want to honor this place?"

"Progress, tribal progress," chanted the trickster. "We learned that the hard way from whites on their way to church."

"But not backwards," said the postman.

"The only way whites let us compete is when we convince them that we're going backward into the future, or when we are sure to lose."

"What's this microlight business?"

"Patronia Microlight Corporation," said the trickster and brushed the dust from his leather trousers. "That's my new ultralight airplane company."

"Wait a minute, do you mean you're going to make those damn noisy things around here?" asked the postman. "No flying around me, never. It's crazy enough around here. You can fetch your mail in town if you're in that business."

"Don't worry, microlights could never be as noisy as that snowmobile you drive, or how about that terrible lawn mower you run every week?"

"Lord, where did you wild people come from anyway?" muttered the bluenose postman. His critical nature was a pose, but at the same time he never trusted people who moved more than once. The tricksters provided him with wild stories, and for that reason he could never avoid the baronage; he would lose his social power in the mail room. "You boys are something, but why can't you be normal like the rest of the Indians around here?"

Slyboots wrote a proposal for federal economic development funds to manufacture microlight airplanes; the review commission ruled that aviation was a frivolous reservation enterprise and denied the plan. The trickster cursed the government for a few hours, and then he rallied with a down-to-earth proposal to build the Microlight Muskeg Rover, a universal terrain vehicle that would crawl through the snow and muck on the reservation.

"Now that makes some sense," said the postman when he delivered the letter that approved the second proposal. "One day, mark my words, you people might put this place together."

The economic development commission was impressed with the terrain vehicle; the concept, movement on oversized tires, was not outside their collective imagination. Within a month the trickster expanded the cedar barn near the pond and installed new tools, equipment, and parts. When he had assembled seven vehicles, the commissioners arrived to witness a test drive in muskeg; the performance was perfect and the commission adopted the project as a model. Politicians and foreign delegations visited the baronage to admire the reservation enterprise; the commission was moved by public relations but incurious that no one ordered the land vehicles; the government, on the other hand, subsidized an imported terrain vehicle from a third world nation that sold for a much lower price. Several months later, when the commission located a new model operation to celebrate, the funds to the baronage were terminated.

"I swear, you people never do anything right," said the postman, a constant critic who was never sentimental. "There goes more taxpayers' money down the old red hole."

Slyboots was ecstatic when the vehicle scheme was terminated because he retained ownership of the parts and equipment; the government had no interest in reclamation on the reservation. The trickster disassembled more than a hundred terrain vehicles, and that winter he built several microlight airplanes with converted snowmobile engines.

The Patronia Microlight was in the air by summer with nineteen orders from four states. The trickster hired women from the scapehouse to assemble the aluminum supports and to sew the nylon flight surfaces while he mounted the engines.

Sister Eternal Flame became the ace microlight test pilot; she circled every lake and cabin on the res ervation that summer. She and her brother delivered the microlights in his biplane. "Slyboots, these airplanes are terrific for us," she shouted to him in the air, "so do something new before you get bored and sell the whole thing out from under us, do you hear me?"

That winter the trickster founded the Patronia Airborne Warriors. He visited public schools on the reservation and told tribal students about his bird hospital in the cities. Those who responded with avian metaphors and visions were invited to train at the international airport on the baronage as airborne tribal warriors. Five women and three men studied aviation and the diseases of common land and water birds. First the students flew in the biplane, and then, later in the summer, they piloted their own microlight back home to visit their families. The response of tribal elders was marvelous; there was as much enthusiasm over tribal aviation and microlights as there was when the trickster started bingo and tribe. The old men heard the engines in the distance and remembered their own avian dreams; a voice that soared with the clouds.

In the second year the demand for microlights more than doubled and the trickster built a new assembly building and a row of apartments on the airport meadow behind the crescent. He had new orders from more than a dozen states and countries.

Griever de Hocus, the mixedblood who taught English at Zhou Enlai University in the People's Republic of China, ordered a microlight to avoid crowded public transportation. Slyboots shipped him two of his best airplanes, one to promote investment in a new peasant market and the other to bribe public officials to release the other microlight. The trickster was right about the bribe and about the peasants; Griever had his microlight and the peasants were eager to fly.

China, his eldest sister, wrote when she was in the People's Republic of China that Griever de Hocus had vanished; he was last seen in the air, over a water park, the police reported, with a rooster and a small blonde. Griever wrote to China that he was on his way south to Macao.

Slyboots and his airborne warriors landed at reservations in several states where the trickster lectured on tribal aviation. The elders were entertained; however, the sentimental liberals were surprised that the trickster had more on his mind than recreational aviation and microlight acrobatics.

"Ten dollars to a doughnut he's moving more than air with those planes of his," said the postman to a scapehouse woman. "The folks in the mail room think he's in the drug business, but I figure he's got a better scheme than that. He knows enough to stay out of jail, and you can say that about all the tricksters here, even that one who sleeps with ladies' shoes."

"Mouseproof Martin?"

"Yes, that's the one," said the postman. "Whatever happened to him? Did he get swallowed up in a giant shoe somewhere?"

The trickster established tribe centers on more than a dozen reservations that summer; he received a small percentage of the operation, a wise move to discourage separations and competition to control the games. He was never troubled with reservation politicians because his percentage was low; even so, he earned much more than he needed to expand his bird hospitals and aviation school.

The following spring he tired of the routine of his aviation enterprises and turned the entire operation over to his sister and the scapehouse women. The trickster and three airborne warriors flew across the Bering Strait to the People's Republic of China; they sold microlights and tribal ginseng and searched for Griever de Hocus.

Ginseng Browne

The MIDDLE KINGDOM
at PATRONIA

Ginseng Browne was born with an instinct to unearth pungent and medicinal roots; as a child he toddled behind his grandmother under the hardwoods in search of garlic and wild ginseng. His natural taste became a business on the baronage.

Ginseng earned an international reputation as a trader in the rare and potent *Panax quinquefolius*, or wild tribal ginseng. Shrewd buyers from Korea, Hong Kong, and the People's Republic of China were astonished that an adolescent mixedblood had the poise and nature to trade the medicinal white roots of heaven on the world market.

The trickster had a wild breath; he was serious, silent most of the time, intense in rooms without windows, and he talked with mongrels. He learned seasoned stories from his grandmother Novena Mae Ironmoccasin; stories on the baronage, and he had no desire to travel outside the reservation where he did not understand the gestures. The world came to his window in search of wild ginseng. The trickster had an unstudied discretion with clever traders on the run.

The trade delegations were eager to control the purchase of the special wild amber ginseng from the baronage; the amber ginseng prepared by the trickster was the most potent, and the most valuable, on the world market.

The United States Department of Agriculture reported that one pound of wild dried ginseng roots from the northern part of the country sold for about sixty-five dollars. The wild amber ginseng from the baronage was traded for more than two hundred dollars a pound.

Ginseng invited three delegates and two translators from the China National Medicine and Health Products Import and Export Corporation of the People's Republic of China to the meadow. The trickster was animated, but he seldom raised his voice above a whisper that afternoon. The mongrels raced in the weeds around the delegates. Chicken Lips barked into panic holes on the meadow rise, and White Lies pushed his wet nose and flews into groins and sneezed.

"How do you find wild ginseng?" asked the senior delegate through a translator. His loose cheeks ballooned when he raised his harsh voice. She Yan, the young translator, had a gentle tone; when she spoke, small beads of perspiration shimmered on her forehead.

"Novena Mea," the trickster whispered.

"Red Indians, are you Catholics?" asked the translator with her head down. Several insects crawled onto her bare legs. The trickster leaned over, touched one finger behind her knee, and teased a ladybug. She Yan pranced in the wild flowers to avoid his hands and the insects.

"My grandmother, she taught me where to find garlic and wild ginseng," said the trickster, as the ladybug marched down his finger with her wings spread wide.

"Red Indians like nature," the translator asserted and wiped her forehead with a small towel. She brushed the back of her knees.

"The Baron of Patronia, my grandfather, grew these flowers with his wild voice," said the trickster. He waved his arms in a wide circle and the mongrels chased butterflies on the meadow.

The Chinese smiled and bowed in the wild flowers; the delegates were patient, but at the same time they were driven to win an exclusive contract to buy the rare and potent amber ginseng that grew on the baronage.

Ginseng was aroused by the attractive translator, but he was evasive, a natural response to negotiations over resources on the reservation. Tribal elders told him stories about the civilized greed that ruined the white pine and cedar and the wild ginseng; immigrant farmers survived by hunting ginseng.

The Chinese wanted all the amber ginseng they could buy on the baronage. The trickster was cordial and generous, but he would not reveal where he found the wild ginseng or how he cured and prepared the valuable amber roots.

The mongrels knew that he gathered the wild roots in the hardwoods near Long Lost Lake where his grandmother once lived. She chewed ginseng there and told stories late at night about the tricksters who became winter birds and the whites who wore black feathers and tried to hide under the trees in the cities.

Ginseng washed the roots with rabbit hair in the warm pond on the baronage. The gentle wash in natural springwater saved the fibrils on the human-shaped ginseng; the roots with clean hair and no bruises were the most valuable. The trickster soaked the ginseng with maple sugar and secret herbs, steamed the roots to a translucent amber hue, and dried them in the late summer sun on rough cedar boards. However, he would never sell this wild ginseng on the world market to the People's Republic of China, or to any other government. The ginseng the trickster negotiated to sell was amber, but the roots would be cultivated on a remote island near the international border.

The Chinese were determined to buy the wild amber, unaware that the trickster planned to trade commercial amber ginseng. The delegates observed that the mixedblood was attracted to the interpreter, so they directed her to establish a trade mission on the baronage.

"Now wait a darn minute," moaned the postman when he heard about the new mission, "this has gone about far enough. You got this scapehouse, and that last tavern, then an international airport, and now, the communist menace right at our back door."

"But this is their homeland," said the trickster.

"Over my dead body," roared the postman.

"The Chinese, you see, are one of the long lost tribes, our brothers," said the trickster with a smile. "You must have heard about the Bering Strait? Well, we migrated from here to there, and now they are coming back. So you see, this is their real homeland."

"My sister told me never to trust a halfbreed," said the postman. "She's right, you people don't care one bit about our country, you would sell us out to the communists in a minute for nothing more than ginseng dust."

"Have you ever taken the train out West?"

"So what?"

"The Chinese built that railroad," said the trickster, who had never been outside the reservation. He imagined time and place and waited for the world to come to him on the baronage.

"That's what I mean," said the postman.

"The whites made us both red."

"I won't touch their mail," shouted the postman as he climbed into the postal truck. He slammed the door and started the engine. "You can tell those reds to get their mail at the main post office."

The Chinese trade mission rented an apartment in the new building at the Patronia International Airport. The delegates visited the baronage three times that summer to continue their negotiations.

Ginseng seemed eager to reach an agreement, but he would alter the proposed contract at the last minute; he was concerned that the mission would be closed and that She Yan, the translator, would be recalled when negotiations were concluded. Meanwhile, the delegation negotiated other contracts with tricksters in the scapehouse and the tavern for birch bark, wild rice, rabbits, chicken feather headdresses, and microlight airplanes.

The People's Republic of China sent a new delegation, their best negotiators, to the baronage when the China National Medicines and Health Products Import and Export Corporation learned that the Bureau of Indian Affairs had been approached by the Republic of China on Taiwan. The delegation did not understand that federal agents had no power on the baronage; however, the trickster did not disabuse them of their concern.

The Chinese negotiators held a banquet on the baronage, honored the trickster with a new name, and proposed the erection of a statue to celebrate the fur trade and mixedbloods on the reservation.

More than a hundred tribal people, and others, including the bluenose postman, were invited to a banquet in an orange circus tent on the meadow. The Chinese served their rich culture in garnished cuisines and in numerous gastronomical combinations: fish, chicken, pheasant, pork tendons, sea slugs, domestic cat, snake, and monkey brains; rice, millet, maize, noodles, and various beans; cabbage, turnips, mushrooms, peaches, pears, and oranges; mountain haw, red pepper, ginger, garlic, and litchi. The tribal elders waited in silence with their hands under the tables; several women whispered about the last tribe winners. The Chinese laced their hands; they were nervous when conversations stopped in the circus tent and no one moved to eat.

"Why does no one eat?" asked She Yan.

"Chopsticks," said Ginseng.

"You teach them how to eat now," she whispered.

"Why not?" he said and cleared his throat to address the crowd in the tent. "The Chinese told me to tell you to eat with your fingers and throw the bones to the mongrels, or you can wait for spoons from the scapehouse."

The negotiators escorted the trickster to the head of the circus tent and announced that the minister of culture was pleased to award him an honorary name. Ginseng was silent; he watched a brown beetle march over the broken weeds.

"Ladies and gentlemen of the White Earth Reservation, barons and tricksters of Patronia," said She Yan. She translated for a woman who represented the minister of culture. "We are honored to present to Ginseng Browne the Chinese name Li Chung Yun in celebration of his wild amber ginseng.

"Ginseng Browne was born in the same year that Li Chung Yun died," said She Yan. She blushed over the praise in translation. "The old man was a famous herbalist who drank ginseng tea and lived to be two-hundred and fifty-six years old."

"Ginseng Li Chung Yun Browne, the mixedblood tribal Monkey King," chanted Sister Eternal Flame. The name was whispered by the scapehouse women.

"The Chinese people and tricksters now come together in this name," said She Yan. "The migration is over, and we have the future to share together at Patronia.

"The minister of culture now dedicates the Trickster of Liberty, a statue to be erected here, on this meadow, where we come together to honor our wild ginseng agreement." The woman unveiled a model of an enormous statue that would be taller than the Statue of Liberty. There were too many toasts that night to celebrate an unsigned agreement.

Ginseng and She Yan walked over the meadow under a whole moon to the shore of Long Lost Lake. There, the trickster told stories about his grandmother who lived alone in a wigwam, and he revealed where the wild ginseng grew. She Yan told stories about the Cultural Revolution and rural factories. The sound of tribe numbers broadcast in the circus tent and excited laughter wavered over the meadow while the trickster and the translator made love on the shoreline.

She Yan was named in the final ginseng contract that was signed later that week; she would remain on the baronage to manage a special trade mission. The negotiators did not know that the amber ginseng would be cultivated on an island near the international border.

The TRICKSTER
of LIBERTY

The Trickster of Liberty, crotch high in copper splendor on
the meadow, cast a low shadow that winter; crows cawed
over the cavernous waist of the abandoned statue.

Ginseng Browne was indicted in federal district
court on seven counts of "international root rustling" and
violations of the endangered species treaties. The China
National Medicines and Health Products Import and Export
Corporation closed their trade mission on the reservation
and ceased construction on the statue to avoid public con-
troversies. The incomplete monument, however, was exposed on television and in newspaper stories.

"Nice banquet, but good riddance, we never
wanted those commies out here in the first place," said the
postman. "That stupid statue, are they leaving that here as a
reminder?"

"They'll be back, they can't do without us here,
they'll be back in no time," the trickster roared and
pounded on the road below the scapehouse. The wild
sound drew women to the windows and crows to the statue.
His hushed and considerate nature had been deposed by
the indictment and the overnight withdrawal of the mission.
Ginseng moved closer to the postman and said, "What
bothers me the most is going to court in the cities." He had
never been outside the reservation; the baronage inspired
his stories and the meadow held his voice.

The federal warrant accused the trickster of stealing
several thousand mature ginseng seeds from a commercial

grower, and with the intent to violate the Convention of International Trade in Endangered Species of Fauna and Flora, a treaty ratified to protect plant and animals species. The Endangered Species Scientific Authority and the United States Fish and Wildlife Service, which oversees the treaty, reported that wild ginseng on the reservation was threatened with extinction because the trickster had agreed to export amber ginseng to the People's Republic of China.

Ginseng imagined that federal court was an urban panic hole, voices buried in cold concrete. He would show his stories but he was not prepared to reveal that his real scheme was to export commercial, not wild, amber ginseng; the tribal trick in his final negotiations. The Chinese closed their trade mission, but they were still eager to trade in amber ginseng.

"Ginseng, you need a lawyer," said the postman.

"No one needs a lawyer."

"Slyboots, he had a lawyer even when he didn't need one."

"He's in China," said the trickster.

"But his lawyer's here."

"Tricksters do better on their own."

"Sue the bastards. Sue the communists to finish that statue and then sell it to some art museum," said the postman as he nodded toward the copper monument. "You could roll it over and turn the hollow into a microlight hanger."

The Trickster of Liberty listed to the right, a natural pose on the meadow. Birds soared between the enormous copper legs, swooped into the vast hollow thighs, but the mongrels and woodland animals would not go near the tarnished statue; their tracks in the snow turned wide around the undone monster.

The scapehouse women watched the sun rise on the

solstices right into the copper crotch of the statue. The old shamans who hummed and rattled and named that place on the meadow where the trickster stands have the last laughs.

Ginseng and She Yan huddled at the window and waited for the sun to break over the cold copper waist. Thin ice slivers had mounted the pane overnight; now the light shivered. They were bound in a blanket, tired and discontent; the trade mission was closed, and she had been ordered to leave the reservation.

"You can't leave now," pleaded Ginseng.

"We are little people," she said.

"We can live back in the woods," said the trickster. He turned from the window. "My grandmother did it, she lived in the woods, and I did it when my brother was killed, and now we can do it too, we don't need to answer to governments."

"But we're in the woods now," said She Yan.

"No, the hardwoods, where the wild ginseng grows."

"What would we eat?"

"Ginseng, of course," he said and smiled. "There's food everywhere. We can eat better in the hardwoods than we can here, believe me."

"My family would be lonesome."

"Yes, but we would be near the baronage."

"Come to China," she whispered.

"No, not now."

"Your brother and sister are there."

"Sometime," he said.

"My mother is alone," said She Yan.

"We could get married," said the trickster as he turned back to the window. Ginseng snorted and then pinched his nose. The sun rose over the copper.

"Ginseng, my visa has expired."

"This is the White Earth Reservation," he said and

raised his voice. "You don't need a visa to be here, we are sovereign." She Yan had a limited diplomatic visa that expired when the trade mission was closed.

"When?" she asked.

"When what?"

"When married?"

"Tonight, tonight!" he shouted and opened his arms. The sunbucked over the pines and warmed the cedar house. He lowered the blanket and touched her shoulders and breasts.

Sister Eternal Flame married Ginseng and She Yan that night, on the winter solstice. The scapehouse women prepared a wild dinner celebration with fresh meats and greens; there were exotic dancers, scented soothsayers, whole moon chanters, and the mongrels were dressed as chamberlain eunuchs. The heirs to the baronage saluted their brothers and sisters.

"Tune, may he rest in peace under a tricorne."

"Tulip, may she whir with a man."

"China, may she bind her lilies," said Sister Flame.

"Slyboots, may he land," said the trickster.

"Father Mother is now a mother and this was his place," said Shadow Box. He tended bar at the reception in the Last Lecture. Wink waited on tables; she smiled and clicked her teeth.

Seven tribal singers whipped a cowboy drum and turned the reception into a powwow dance that lasted until dawn. The mongrels howled and barked around the drum in the center of the tavern. Some celebrants lost their names that winter night, but there was only one last lecture and a new name.

She Yan Browne held the microphone in her small hands and confessed that her first impressions of the baronage were not positive. "These dogs, we would eat them at home, and all those mosquitoes bothered me too much," she said and laughed. Her voice hissed over the loudspeaker. "We were taught that Red Indians were primitives and savages, but you people are all mixed up like television."

"Mixedblood is the word," whispered Ginseng.

"Yes, mixedbloods are all mixed up in a television movie," she said and nodded to her husband. "We never knew that you mixedbloods were the real Red Indians."

"No one is a real Indian," shouted an elder at the bar.

"We found out about that, and then I felt much better," she said and sighed. "Ginseng, he is a wonder man and here we are together and now I got a new name, you bet your boots, is that what to say?"

Shadow Box, Wink, Sister Eternal Flame, and several shamans agreed that night to adopt She Yan as an heir to the baronage and a tribal member of the White Earth Reservation.

"This is her original homeland," said See See Arachnidan, the trickster geneticist who was elected to announce the tribal adoption. "She Yan Browne is back with us now, after a long migration, an heir to the sovereign baronage."

Patronia was a tribal sanctuary; federal agents tried to enforce immigration laws on the reservation, but the courts ruled that tribal members had a sovereign and inalienable right to live on land established in treaties.

She Yan carried a map of the reservation so that she would never cross the border by accident and risk arrest by immigration officers; she memorized the names of border towns and measured the miles between communities. She was more aware of her environment than she had ever been back home.

Ginseng had never been outside the reservation and She Yan could not leave; he was unnerved because the court hearing was in the cities. Sovereign imagination and mixed-blood tribal identities are enlaced with unusual limitations and political ironies.

Sister Eternal Flame came to the rescue once more; she and two other scapehouse women decided to attend the hearing dressed in wimples, veils, and black habits. She Yan was disguised as a solemn nun to leave the reservation. The four sisters sat in the back row of the courtroom.

Ginseng listened to the federal prosecutor accuse him of various species crimes, and then he turned his head from side to side and raised his hand to attract the attention of the judge. The trickster pretended that he spoke only a tribal language, and through an interpreter he asked the court to provide translators. This delayed the hearing for several weeks and put the prosecutor on the defensive because he could not find a tribal person willing to serve the government as an interpreter. At last he enlisted a proud anthropologist and the hearing was resumed.

Ginseng heard the prosecutor and then the anthropologist, but he pretended to listen to his own translator, a shaman from Bad Medicine Lake. The prosecutor said the trickster had stolen ginseng seeds and had violated the endangered species export laws. The trickster, in his time, told stories about conversations he imagined between whites and tribal elders who had agreed that the tribe held the sovereign right to hunt, fish, and gather ginseng and other natural herbs; these rights were protected in treaties.

The federal judge instructed the trickster, in translation, that his stories were no more than hearsay evidence, "We can listen to you, and what you know, but we cannot consider what you heard other men say, other men who are now dead."

Ginseng paused, pretended not to understand the judge, and then said, through his shaman translator, "If you don't believe what tribal people say in my stories, then I don't believe what whites have said in those stories printed in your law books."

The audience in the courtroom cheered and applauded the trickster; the oral tradition was precedent in imagination. The judge leaned forward with his head in his hands. "You can say that again," he muttered and then instructed the prosecutor to continue.

"We have written evidence that this man agreed to export wild amber ginseng, an endangered species, to the People's Republic of China," said the prosecutor in translation. The anthropologist spoke in a clear tone, but his facial expressions and hand movements were cultural contradictions to the tribal meaning of the words.

Behind the scenes there were international political and economic schemes that would, in the end, determine the outcome of the trial to protect an endangered species. The Republic of China on Tiawan pressured the Bureau of Indian Affairs to obstruct tribal negotiations with the People's Republic of China and other communist nations. Hong Kong traders, meanwhile, were in competition with other governments and bribed public officials to gain control of reservation ginseng. Korean, Japanese, and Canadian traders were also in the courtroom.

Ginseng argued through the shaman that he had a tribal right to gather ginseng. "Ginseng was used in traditional tribal ceremonies, and our right to use eagle feathers and ginseng is protected under the tribal religious freedom act," said the trickster.

"What ceremonials?" asked the anthropologist.

"Grand Medicine Society."

"That's very interesting," the anthropologist mused with his narrow thumb on his mustache. "I don't recall that Walter Hoffman had anything to say about ginseng in his report 'The Midewiwin, or Grand Medicine Society.' "

"Hoffman invented Indians. He was scared," shouted the trickster in a tribal language. "He's your authority not ours, we practice with ease what he envied and tried to own."

"Please continue," said the judge.

"But even so, you're wrong because Hoffman stole ginseng and published our stories about how ginseng was used to heal and prolong life," said the trickster. "He stole our stories and wrote, 'The Mide spirit taught us to do right. He gave us life and told us how to prolong it. These things he taught us and gave us roots for medicine.' "

"Do you have a citation?" asked the anthropologist.

"We have the right to ginseng because we are sovereign," the trickster replied and turned his back on the anthropologist. "We have a right to the seeds because of our tribal ceremonies."

"But not to steal the seeds from a commercial grower or to export an endangered species," the prosecutor said as he turned a pencil in his hand. "Furthermore, your honor, this man hired three white men to steal the seeds from a ginseng farm in Marathon County, Wisconsin. Mister Ginseng, please enlighten the court, How is theft a religious experience?"

"Whites are the thieves," said the shaman.

"We have a religious right to ginseng no matter where it grows," said the trickster. "Whites have no rights to our wild ginseng."

The judge ruled that the federal government had jurisdiction over the ginseng matter and a trial was scheduled in the spring. She Yan, Sister Eternal Flame, and the other sisters moaned and pounded their black oxfords on the floor.

The People's Republic of China kept a diplomatic distance from the reservation; at the same time, there was political pressure to reopen their trade mission on the reservation. Communist agents spied on the heirs to the baron-age and reported on the activities of the trickster. The China National Medicines and Health Products Import and Export Corporation maintained an interest in wild tribal ginseng and the negotiated agreement with the trickster.

The Hong Kong traders were in competition for reservation ginseng; they hired private investigators and a public relations organization to gather intelligence on com-munist influences on reservations and to influence public opinion in favor of free trade. The reservation postman was even paid for information. The traders wanted to deal with the trickster and supported his sovereign claim to wild gin-seng. Hong Kong has been the leading trader in world ginseng, but now, since the United States China Trade Agreement, the People's Republic of China has become more aggressive in the market.

The Republic of China on Taiwan lobbied national leaders and state representatives to oppose the communists on the baronage. Special agents enlisted the postman as an informer and worked with the Bureau of Indian Affairs to gather information that would support the government prosecutor in court. The Republic of China was not inter-ested in reservation ginseng but denied tribal sovereignty to terminate communist negotiations on the reservation; the argument was ideological not economic.

The Endangered Species Scientific Authority and the United States Fish and Wildlife Service were the over-seers of the international treaty ratified to protect animals and plant species; the overseers were idealistic and not interested in tribal ceremonies, ideologies, or ginseng eco-nomics. They argued that tribal sovereignty did not exclude the tribes from the international endangered species treaty.

"She's dressed like a nun," the postman whispered

to the traders, who paid him the most to inform on the tricksters. "Watch out for the penguins," he told the agents from the Bureau of Indian Affairs.

Sister Eternal Flame and She Yan wore habits to various events in small towns near the reservation; their disguises seemed so natural that the sisters were casual and unconcerned. Late one afternoon agents from the Bureau of Indian Affairs and spies from the Republic of China seized the nuns outside the reservation; the sisters had been at a supermarket. She Yan and Sister Flame were covered and tied in the back of a van; minutes later more than a dozen agents hired by the Hong Kong traders surrounded the vehicle and liberated the sisters. Back on the reservation, the traders explained that they would protect the nuns and defend their sovereign claims for a contract to buy wild amber ginseng from the baronage. "If I win my trial, you've got a deal," said the trickster.

Ginseng insisted that his trial begin on the vernal equinox; the first daffodils and blues were in bloom on the meadow when federal court convened in the cities. The trickster elected to argue before a judge not a jury.

The judge read the indictments, and then the government prosecutor, with his anthropologist as translator, described the endangered herbal root and reviewed the history of wild ginseng.

"Ginseng, which means 'man essence' is a root, a medicinal herb that is believed to be a stimulant, antidiabetic, and carminative tonic. This herb is native to hardwood forests, such as those on the White Earth Reservation.

"Ginseng blooms in midsummer and matures in about seven years," said the prosecutor. "The flowers are greenish yellow with bright crimson berries in late summer and autumn. The roots are forked with circular wrinkles."

"Have you ever tasted ginseng?" asked the trickster through the shaman. He placed a small brown carton in the center of the table.

"No, taste is not the point here."

"Have you ever seen ginseng?"

"Objection, your honor," said the prosecutor.

"Here's some real wild ginseng from the baronage," said the trickster as he opened the carton and arranged seven amber human-shaped roots in a circle on the table. The transluscent amber shimmered on the dark wood.

"Please continue," said the judge.

"In the first half of the eighteenth century, there was an immoderate harvesting, a boom in the wild ginseng harvest in French Canada. Then, late in the eighteenth century, ginseng was exported for the first time to China from the United States by John Jacob Astor. Wild ginseng then, and commercial ginseng now, has been related to the fur trade.

"Gordon Patty, in the article, 'United States Ginseng in the Far East Market' published by the Department of Agriculture, writes that ginseng was 'first gathered by French trappers and Indians and shipped from Canada via Europe and also from New England. The ultimate destination was China. Beginning mainly after the Revolutionary War . . . pioneers and their descendants looked for ginseng all through the hilly, wooded sections of eastern states. It was considered a good source of cash when other crops failed,' " said the prosecutor.

"Patty went on to say that the 'growing scarcity of American ginseng as the great virgin forests were cut, accompanied by higher prices, led to commercial cultivation of the plant, beginning in the late nineteenth century. Toward the end of the century, ginseng cultivation was a boom industry,' " said the prosecutor. The anthropologist cleared his throat and continued his translation. "He wrote, 'But overexpansion resulted in overproduction, and by 1904 disease became severe and much of the seed crop was destroyed.'

"Ginseng Browne stole commercial seeds and he harvests wild ginseng on the reservation for export," said the prosecutor. The anthropologist smiled as he translated. "Indians, as history has shown, are part of the problem and sovereignty is not an excuse to bring this herb to extinction. The international endangered species treaty must be upheld even on reservations."

"The problem's pure white," shouted the trickster. "Ginseng was lost because whites cut the hardwoods and not because we harvested a few roots. Whites stole the hardwoods, our ginseng, and they even stole our stories."

"Ginseng Browne has violated sections of the Convention of International Trade in Endangered Species of Fauna and Flora treaty, which was ratified by the United States," the prosecutor recited. "The harvest of wild ginseng for export violates the treaty because the root is threatened with extinction."

Ginseng would never reveal that he intended to export commercial amber ginseng; to do that would eliminate his chances to trade with the People's Republic of China. The potent wild ginseng was consumed on the baronage. He mounted a defense based on the American Indian Religious Freedom Act and claimed that he had a sovereign tribal right to ginseng roots and seeds. When the trickster learned that one commercial grower had stolen tribal land to raise ginseng, he hired three whites to rustle the seeds, a sovereign right to what grows on treaty land.

"Your Honor," pleaded the trickster, "we would like to demonstrate that wild ginseng is used by shamans to cure various diseases."

"Why?" asked the judge.

"To show the religious power of wild ginseng."

"Objection, Your Honor,"

"Continue with your ginseng show," said the judge.

"First, we have a tribal man with white hair," said the trickster. "Now, watch his hair darken as he chews one small amber root." The man chewed and his hair turned darker.

"Objection, Your Honor."

"Please, continue," the judge shouted as he brushed his thin white hair with his hands. "Would you submit some of that ginseng as an exhibit?"

"Now, Your Honor, we have four tribal men who will drink amber ginseng tea to improve their sexual performance." The men supped the hot tea and four women in the back of the courtroom shouted their endorsement.

"Here we have an old tribal woman on crutches and with no teeth," said the trickster as he guided the women forward to the bench. He told her in a whisper to smile. "There, nothing but gums, and she is crippled, almost blind, but when she chews ginseng nothing will be the same again." The old woman chewed a stout amber root and threw her glasses across the courtroom; then she slammed one of her crutches on the table. "There, see, the amber ginseng has made her teeth grow again, and look, she can walk, she can walk and talk." The woman raised her second crutch and moved closer to the bench.

The judge declared a recess and ducked his head as the old woman waved her crutch. She cursed the laws that allowed whites to steal tribal land and cut the trees on reservations, but the closer she came to the bench the more she smiled; when the judge winked and smiled back, the woman dropped the crutch and strutted out the back of the courtroom.

See See Arachnidan released nine parasitic testicle ticks when the trial resumed; she had engineered the ticks to seek the groin sweat of authoritarian personalities. One bite and the men started to stutter. The officers of the court, the government prosecutor, and the anthropologist scratched and stuttered, so the judge declared a second recess. See See whistled and the testicks crawled back into the leather pouch that hung over her shoulder.

Meanwhile, during the two recesses, a clever compromise was proposed that the federal prosecutor would not refuse. The People's Republic of China agreed to buy ginseng seed instead of the amber roots, which is what they wanted in the first place. The Hong Kong traders would have what they thought was the wild ginseng, and the Republic of China, with the Bureau of Indian Affairs, would take credit for exposing a communist threat on a reservation.

"We have a right to the ginseng seeds," said the trickster to the prosecutor as he poured sugar into his coffee. The interested parties gathered in a basement restaurant. "Honor our sovereign rights to the seeds and we got a deal."

"Wait a minute, what's that?" asked the anthropologist.

"What, sugar?"

"So, you understand after all," said the prosecutor as he paced around the table with his hands buried in his suit coat pockets. "You never did need a translator."

"He's a trickster," said the anthropologist.

"We want the seeds," said a trade representative from the People's Republic of China. "We buy the seeds and that would be fine."

"We want the wild ginseng," said the traders from Hong Kong. "We pay the highest prices and we are the largest traders in the world."

"Now that sounds like a deal to me," said the trickster. The shaman translated everything he heard into a tribal language. "Drop all the charges and we got a deal."

"The judge will decide," muttered the prosecutor.

"Wait, there's one more thing," said the trickster with his hands raised. "She Yan must run the trade mission again, and then we got a whole deal."

Ginseng would buy commercial ginseng with the money he made from the sale of the seeds; and with maple sugar and herbs, his secret preparation, the trickster would turn the white human shapes into amber roots for the Hong Kong traders. The potent wild amber ginseng would remain on the baronage.

The delegation from the China National Medicines and Health Products Import and Export Corporation invited See See Arachnidan to become a citizen of China. She gathered her testicks, delivered her last lecture in the marble rotunda of the federal courthouse, and selected a new name. The Chinese were so eager to obtain the parasitic testicle ticks that they promised to complete the Trickster of Liberty statue on the baronage. When these agreements between traders, spies, agents, shamans, sisters, heirs, and a wild genetics engineer were presented to the judge, he cleared his throat, pocketed the wild ginseng evidence, and dismissed the charges against the trickster. The nuns undressed in the back of the courtroom, and the mongrels barked on the meadow.

Epilogue

LOSS LEADERS from the UNIVERSITIES

Milan Kundera said in an interview in *Salmagundi* that the "novelist is neither historian nor prophet: he is an explorer of existence." The novelist continues a comic discourse that overturns historicism and representations; the trickster arises as an usher in an existential language game. Imagination, in this sense, is dissidence, and the trickster is liberation.

Julia Kristeva pointed out that "our present age is one of exile. . . . Exile is already in itself a form of *dissidence,* since it involves uprooting oneself from a family, a country or a landscape." She argued that *thought* continues to be the "true dissidence" and distinguishes three types of dissident. The first is the "rebel who attacks political power" but paranoia limits him to the dialectic of the master and slave. The second is the "psychoanalyst who transforms the dialectic of law-and-desire into a contest between *death and discourse.*" The third dissident is the "writer who experiments with the limits of identity, producing texts where the law does not exist outside language." The tribal trickster liberates the mind in a comic discourse that reveals new signs, identities, and uncertain humor.

Sergeant Alex Hobraiser and Doctor Eastman Shicer provided these notes to a comic discourse on the trickster: "It's Time for a Change In Our Change," by Ed Reiter, *New York Times*, Sunday, May 3, 1987; *Cesar Vellejo: The Dialectics of Poetry and Silence*, by Jean Franco; N. Scott Momaday, quoted in *Wordarrows*, by Gerald Vizenor; *The Trickster: A Study in American Indian Mythology*, by Paul Radin; *The Trickster in West Africa: A Study of Mythic Irony and Sacred Delight*, by Robert Pelton; *Women, Androgynes, and Other Mythical Beats*, by Wendy Doniger O'Flaherty; *Toward a Rocognition of Androgyny*, by Carolyn Heilbrun; *Lectures on the I Ching: Constancy and Change*, by Richard Wilhelm; *And Our Faces, My Heart Brief as Photos*, by John Berger; "On the Psychology of the Trickster Figure," by Carl Gustav Jung, in *The Trickster*, by Paul Radin; *The Comedy of Survival: Studies in Literary Ecology*, by Joseph Meeker; *The Four Fundamental Concepts of Psychoanalysis*, by Jacques Lacan; *Figuring Lacan: Criticism and the Cultural Unconsciousnes*, by Juliet Flower MacCannell; *The Cosmic Web*, by N. Katherine Hayles; *Women, Fire, and Dangerous Things*, by George Lakoff; *The Kristeva Reader*, edited by Toril Moi. Roland Barthes was interviewed by Philip Brook in *Le Nouvel Observateur* and later published in *The Grain of the Voice*. Michel Foucault is quoted from his introduction to *Herculine Barbin: Being the Recently Discovered Memoirs of a Ninteenth-Century French Hermaphrodite*.

The quotations on land allotment in the first chapter of this novel are from an original patent issued to Alice Beaulieu, my paternal grandmother, a White Earth Mississippi Chippewa Indian. The patent was issued by order of the secretary of the interior and signed by President Theodore Roosevelt on May 21, 1908.

Griever de Hocus first appeared in the novel *Griever: An American Monkey King in China,* by Gerald Vizenor. The conception of the mind monkey or monkey king is from *The Journey to the West,* translated by Anthony C. Yu, and *Monkey,* translated by Arthur Waley.

Roy Wagner wrote in *The Invention of Culture* that Ishi "brought the world into the museum." Ishi, the last survivor of the Yahi tribe, was "discovered" in 1911. Alfred Kroeber, then chairman of the Department of Anthropology and curator of the Museum of Anthropology and Ethnology, housed his tribal friend in the museum at the University of California.

The idea of transvaluation of the despised is borrowed from *The Broken Covenant,* by Robert Bellah. Ideas from these authors were also mentioned in the trickster stories: *The Cart That Changed the World,* by Terry Wilson; "Socioacupuncture: Mythic Reversals and the Striptease in Four Scenes," by Gerald Vizenor, in *The American Indian and the Problem of History,* edited by Calvin Martin; *The Vanishing Race and Other Illusions,* by Christopher Lyman; "Earth-Diver: Creation of the Mythopoeic Male," by Alan Dundas, reprinted in *Sacred Narrative*; "Bone Courts," by Gerald Vizenor, *American Indian Quarterly; History of the Ojibway Nation,* by William Warren; *Ishi in Two Worlds,* by Theodora Kroeber; "The Mide wiwin; or 'Grand Medicine Society' of the Ojibwa," by Walter Hoffman, United States Bureau of Ethnology; "United States Ginseng in the Far East Market," by Gordon Patty, United States Department of Agriculture.

References to President William McKinley, the anarchist Leon Czolgosz, and Theodore Roosevelt, who named a tribal child born at the Pan-American Exposition, are from *All the World's a Fair: Visions of Empire at American International Expositions, 1876-1916*, by Robert Rydell.

Sister Eternal Flame, Benito Saint Plumero, and the mongrels Private Jones and Pure Gumption, first appeared at the Scapehouse on Callus Road in the novel *Darkness in Saint Louis Bearheart*, by Gerald Vizenor. Doc Cloud Burst, creator of the San Francisco Sun Dancers, Sarah Blue Welcome, Token White, and others, appeared in "Monsignor Missalwait's Interstate," by Gerald Vizenor, in *The New Native American Novel.*

Gerald
VIZENOR

Gerald Vizenor, a mixedblood member of the Minnesota
Chippewa tribe, is a professor of literature and American
Studies at the University of California, Santa Cruz. He has
also taught at the University of California, Berkeley, the
University of Minnesota and Tianjin University in China.
Vizenor wrote the original screenplay for *Harold of Orange*,
which won the Film-in-the-Cities National screenwriting
award and was also named "Best Film" at the San Francisco
American Indian Film Festival. His second novel, *Griever:
An American Monkey King in China*, won the New York
Fiction Collective Prize and the American Book Award
sponsored by the Before Columbus Foundation.

Vizenor has published several collections of haiku
poems; *Matsushima: Pine Island* is the most recent. Selec-
tions of his poems and short stories have appeared in several
anthologies, including *Voices of the Rainbow* and *Words in
the Blood*. The University of Minnesota Press has published
three of his books on the American Indian experience:
Wordarrows, Earthdivers, and *The People Named the
Chippewa*.